D1361983

Skin

Skin

sensual tales by

Catherine Hiller

HILLE

Carroll & Graf Publishers, Inc.
New York

First Carroll & Graf edition 1997

Carroll & Graf Publishers, Inc.
260 Fifth Avenue
New York, NY 10001

Library of Congress Cataloging-in-Publication Data

Hiller, Catherine.
    Skin: sensual tales / by Catherine Hiller. — 1st Carroll & Graf
ed.
        p.   cm.
    ISBN 0–7867–0436–7 (paper)
    1. Erotic stories, American.   I. Title.
PS3558.I4458S58   1997
813'.54—dc21
                                                                97–2041
                                                                   CIP

Manufactured in the United States of America

Publication history for the stories in *Skin*:

"Skin" and "My Lover's Family" won PEN/NEA Syndicated Fiction Awards.

"The February Fantasy" and "The Perfect Aphrodisiac" were first published in *Penthouse*.

"Bad Sex" appeared in the anthology *Bad Sex* (Serpent's Tail, 1993) under the title "Some Rules About Adultery."

"Boss Lady" appeared, somewhat differently, in the novel *17 Morton Street* (St. Martin's Press, 1990).

acknowledgments

I am grateful to the men who inspired the stories in this collection: Antoine, Lenny, Malcolm, Mark, Peter, Peter, and Stan.

I am lucky to have Jane DeLynn as a critic and a friend.

I am thankful to the Yaddo Corporation for its generosity.

And I am very glad Susan Schulman persisted.

To Mark

contents

Bad Sex

HE WAS SHORT, CHUNKY, BALDING, bespectacled—not at all the kind of man Daria flirted with at parties. Yet here she was again, off in an intimate corner with Henry at another of Bettina's soirees.

Henry Pomeranz, a divorced professor of anthropology, was one of Bettina's old boyfriends. Daria had known him a little for years and thought he was intelligent, cultured, good-hearted—and nerdy. So it always amazed her how a few words from him could make her shine and blush.

In their alcove, Henry said, "I like you with your hair like that. It's nice to see the shape of your face."

Daria had put her hair up with a barrette because of the heat of the party. Now she could feel that some of the hair in the back had come down. Thick strands lay on her neck, like limp lily leaves. She said, "It's falling."

"I'll put it back up for you."

She looked past him in their alcove and into the rest of the room. She couldn't see her husband, Lewis.

Daria and Lewis had been married twenty years. She was forty-three, with large brown eyes, a wide jaw, and a slender body; she had often been told she looked like a dancer. He was tall and lean, clean-shaven, so you could see all the beautiful bones in his face.

In the next room, people were dancing. Daria thought Lewis was probably there.

"I'm good with hair," said Henry, coming closer.

Daria said nothing. Henry opened the barrette, and her hair tumbled down. He watched it fall, then ran his fingers from her scalp to the ends of her hair. Again and again, he moved his fingers through her hair, as if combing it out. She stayed very still, because his hands on her head and along her hair were like hot winds running down her body. Her head drooped, like an overblown rose, and he gathered her hair and gently tugged it upward to look at her. Then he let all her smooth hair fall to her shoulders again. "Have to start over," he murmured, and she felt every tendril glowing yes toward him.

"I must be very drunk," she lied, closing her eyes and drifting into space under his hands.

"What's going on here?" asked Bettina.

Daria opened her eyes. The good thing was, Henry didn't stop fiddling with her hair so nothing seemed covert and she could keep on enjoying his touch. Now that her eyes were open, Daria found that she could think and she could talk. She said to Bettina, "Henry's being good enough to help me with my hair."

He clipped the barrette closed and said, "That should do it." In parting, he gave the back of her neck a short, transcendent caress.

"Wow," said Bettina. "How long has this been going on?"

Henry Pomeranz replied, "It's just beginning, isn't it, Daria?"

"*What?*" Daria felt stupid, speechless, both ways dumb, pink with shame and joy. How could he know her excitement? She had been so quiet.

"I'm getting another glass of wine," he said, grinning, moving past them. "Can I get you anything?"

The women shook their heads. When he had gone, Bettina said to Daria, "Are you interested?"

Daria said nothing.

"I know he thinks you're hot." Bettina tossed her dark hair back and looked into Daria's eyes. Bettina's eyes glowed turquoise. She said, "You might be great together."

Since Bettina's marriage to Bernie the year before, she and Henry had become the best of friends. They walked and took bike rides together. He baby-sat for her little son. He told her all about his love life. If Henry had an extra ticket, he would take Bettina to a concert or the theater. He and Bernie went to basketball games together.

"Really," said Bettina, managing to speak sotto voce over the noise of her party, "You should think about it with Henry."

Swaying slightly from the afterglow of Henry's hands, Daria wondered why Bettina was urging him on her. Perhaps she wanted to be in the middle, the confidante of both.

Daria found herself saying to Bettina, "This is not a good time for me to have an affair. Lewis and I have been quarreling." As a long-married woman with a sulky daughter of sixteen, Daria sometimes enjoyed shocking her newly married friend. Now Daria pronounced, "I would only start an affair if things were going well with Lewis."

When it came time to leave, Daria looked for Henry so she could say good-bye and give this stubby man an excuse to lay hands on her again, but she couldn't find him anywhere.

* * *

Three weeks went by before Henry Pomeranz called. By then, Daria had almost forgotten about his hands on her hair, and she and Lewis had stopped fighting. When things were going well at work, Lewis became altogether better-natured. Once again, it was clear to Daria that she and Lewis had a strong and happy marriage, so she agreed to meet Henry at the Museum of Modern Art the following Tuesday.

Daria had some rules about adultery. She would never fool around with a friend or an associate of Lewis's. She never made a date unless Lewis was at work so she could say to herself that she wasn't depriving him of anything, really. And she always hid her trysts without ever having to lie. As a fund-raiser for a large theater company, Daria spent hours away from the office, seeing people. She could easily spend time with a lover—although she hadn't done so since breaking up with Pierre two years before.

Now she had Tuesday to think about. Henry had told her that he didn't teach on Tuesday. God, would she soon know his schedule, his telephone number, and his apartment as well as she knew her own?

Meeting him at the museum was initially deflating. He was shorter and plainer than she had remembered. He did not greet her romantically: he shook her hand hello. He was wearing a rumpled oxford shirt and blue jeans neither sexily tight nor fashionably baggy. She thought, this is a man with zero pizzazz.

They wandered through the permanent collection, point-ing out their favorite paintings. They turned a corner and she said, "Where's the Manet that was here?"

"I think it's out on loan."

Daria said, "They shouldn't take away my friends without consulting me." She wondered if this didn't sound too cute, but he seemed charmed, he was smiling at her.

"They're better than friends," he said, "because they don't change. We never want our friends to change, do we?"

This had not occurred to her, and seemed true, and she looked at him thoughtfully.

"How long were you married?" she asked suddenly.

"Eighteen years. And I've been divorced five. Are you happily married?"

"Mostly."

"We had an open marriage," he said.

"I don't," said Daria.

"I can respect that. Are you ready for some lunch?"

In the museum dining room, Daria told Henry a bit about her happy marriage. "I always find Lewis interesting," she said. "And we enjoy our lives together. We're lucky, I guess."

She did not tell him that over the course of her happy marriage she had also had four lovers. In her sudden conviction that she could never sleep with Henry because he wasn't good-looking enough, Daria said, "Lewis is smart, he's dynamic, he's hardworking, and he's funny."

"That's all very nice," said Henry Pomeranz, "but does Lewis worship your body?"

He put his hand on her forearm. A hot wind hit her chest and left her breathless, smiling wordlessly.

"What's so funny?" he asked.

"Lewis and I have passed the worship stage."

"That's a pity," said Henry. He grazed his fingers from her elbow to her wrist and then ran them lightly up again. He stuck his thumb deep into the inner crook of her elbow. Her arm, she now realized, had become an erogenous zone, and he was giving it to her, filling her up. Her breath came fast.

Henry smiled and withdrew his hand. "Think about it," he said. "I have to go."

"Yes, I have to go too." Daria stood up with difficulty.

She was insanely turned on. It made no sense. What did he have, anyway? Magic fingers?

After they parted—she insisted on putting her mouth upon his—she turned around to look at him. A short, chunky man in a rumpled shirt was walking away from her with a bounce in his step.

Another of Daria's adultery rules involved a waiting period, so the following Tuesday they met at the Brooklyn Botanical Gardens. The cherry blossoms were out—if a little past peak—and Daria and Henry walked on a carpet of petals.

"I wish you were married," said Daria.

Henry asked, "Why is that?"

"It would make it more even between us. We'd want the same things. I wouldn't worry about . . ."

"What?"

"Oh, things." It seemed immodest to say she wouldn't worry about him falling in love with her—and premature to say she didn't want him single, out there, meeting other women. Married lovers were best for many reasons. Pierre had been married, and so had the other three.

Four affairs over twenty years wasn't so terrible, was it? Though Lewis would certainly think so, unless he'd had affairs of his own. She never asked. Either way, she knew she'd feel bad.

"I'm not married now," said Henry Pomeranz, "but I know how it is. I'd be careful. I'm a player."

His eyes looked small and glittery behind his thick glasses. He moved closer to her under the cherry blossoms. But instead of kissing her, he reached for her head. He pressed his thumbs in the space between her eyebrows and circled there slowly. The tips of his fingers played in her hair. She felt his strong, gentle hands soothing her, smoothing her, stroking her brain.

Daria had never known a man, married or not, with hands as good as this. She swayed against him. He patted her behind. Soon she felt she had a second brain down there.

"Next Tuesday," he said, "we'll meet in my apartment."

Both her brains agreed.

"So what's going on between you and Henry?" asked Bettina at lunch the next day. They were in a coffee shop eating turkey sandwiches. Bettina taught English at a college near Daria's office.

"What does Henry say?" asked Daria.

Bettina said, "He says he's seeing you, nothing more."

"There's not much more to say." Only Henry's hands on her for a few seconds here and there. "He wants to 'worship my body,'" Daria couldn't help adding. "Maybe someday I'll let him."

Bettina shook her head and frowned at her forkful of coleslaw.

Daria asked, "What is it?"

"I thought I'd enjoy this more than I do."

Daria grinned. "That's life," she said. "Ever surprising. You didn't, I gather, find anything unusual about Henry's hands?"

Bettina shook her head again. "I'll look at them next time I see him."

Daria tried to recall what Henry's hands looked like. She smiled as she realized she hadn't a clue.

"You're no fun when you're like this," grumbled Bettina. "All grinning and silent. And Henry's the same way. Instead of knowing everything about your affair, or whatever it is, I know nothing!"

"People aren't puppets," said Daria. "You can't always pull all the strings."

*　　*　　*

It was too warm for a jacket, so Henry couldn't help her off with anything, so he had no excuse to touch her on greeting. "Hello, hello," he said, grinning. He showed her his place. It was a pleasant apartment midtown. They ended the tour in the living room. A little feast was spread upon the coffee table near the couch. Small bowls held taramasalata, babaganoush, olives, dried figs, fresh strawberries, white cheese. Pita bread and Russian rye lay on a cutting board. There were two wineglasses and an open bottle of Beaujolais.

"Are you thirsty?" asked Henry, and she nodded and drank. Then she found herself eating voraciously. Henry sipped his wine and watched her.

"So good!" she said. "Delicious."

She dipped a piece of pita into the babaganoush and pronounced, "This is my favorite kind of eating. Little rich hors d'oeuvres."

She reached for a dried fig. Would she ever stop eating? He wasn't making it easy by not touching her. If he wasn't going to touch her, what was she doing here at all? She took a second fig.

"Do you always eat like this?" he asked with a smile.

"It's all so good. And maybe I'm nervous." She considered what next to put in her mouth. She placed a chunk of cheese on a piece of rye and brought it to her lips. She took a bite.

"Don't be nervous," said Henry, touching her forehead.

At once, eating was impossible. The bread and cheese turned to clay in her mouth. She spat them discreetly onto a napkin and turned toward Henry.

He tortured her. He stroked her head for ten minutes before doing anything else, and then he spent even longer massaging the back of her neck.

Hot, damp, trembling, Daria finally croaked, "Maybe we should go to your bedroom."

He chuckled. "If you like."

She took off all her clothes and lay on his white sheets awaiting him. He took off his clothes too. He had such a thick mat of hair on his chest, it was like fur. His chest itself was round and soft around the nipples, so from a certain angle it looked like he had furry breasts.

This was Daria's last coherent thought for some time.

Paunchy Henry Pomeranz brought her bliss upon bliss.

Daria had always enjoyed making love with her handsome husband, and her previous lovers, but Henry pleased her more than anybody ever had. She wanted whatever he did, even if she'd never thought of it before.

He pinched her lightly down low.

He placed her legs in a strange position so that he and she made an X and their heads were far apart.

He wet his index finger and placed it where they were conjoined.

She moaned, she screamed, she wept.

Sometimes she looked at him. Invariably, his eyes were closed and he was smiling, Buddha-like, utterly serene, as if he'd found a sacred place.

In the next few weeks Daria noticed that in New York City there were many men who looked something like Henry. Whenever she saw one of his tribe, chunky men of middle age with beards, she would examine him closely and wonder about him in bed. Twice, she'd been startled when a Henry look-alike had returned her hungry gaze. Being in love with Henry left her open to a whole new range of men.

"What's going on?" asked Bettina one day on the phone. "I've never seen Henry so happy."

Daria gave a giggle.

Bettina said, "What is it? Just sex?"

"Uh-huh."

There was a pause, then Bettina burst out, "I don't get it! I don't remember anything special about him!"

"I find him just perfect."

"He's not real big or anything."

"That's true."

"And he's not all that virile."

Their first afternoon together, Henry and Daria had made love four times. But she didn't want to compare notes with Bettina, so Daria just said, "I'd rather be in bed with Henry Pomeranz than doing anything else in the world."

"I don't believe this," said Bettina in exasperation.

Daria took pity on her friend. She said, "Remember my clitoris aphorism?"

"Vaguely. Say it again."

"The trouble with men," Daria pronounced, "is they either don't know where the clitoris is—or they do."

"Then they get too direct and insistent," said Bettina, "so it hurts or it tickles."

"That's right."

Bettina asked, "How does this apply to Henry?"

"That's the thing," said Daria. "It doesn't."

Daria had written poetry in high school and stories in college, and now she wrote grants as part of her job. But she had never before felt moved to write a myth, not even mentally. Now, during the slow times of her day, on the street or before sleep or in the car with Lewis, she found herself constructing a story to account for Henry's talents—especially his skill with his hands. For he was good with his mouth and good with his cock and good with positions and ideas. But he was utterly fantastic with his hands. And as she wondered why, she felt in her bones what she had learned theoretically at college: that mystery begets myth and that the need to explain fires fiction.

One afternoon at the office, Daria wrote down the myth

she had made. She gave it to him on his birthday. As he read, a smile came and went upon his face.

In the myth, Henry arrives at his office early one morning and discovers a beautiful woman going through his files. Introducing herself as "V," she says she wants to read his notes on an ancient sex manual he is decoding. In return, she offers him a hand-drawn map of a township in northern Ontario. She says, "Bathe in the waters of this pond and you will always be happy in love." "Nonsense!" he says, and starts to call campus security. She disappears, leaving the map. Three years later, on a whim, leaving for a lecture in Toronto, he brings along the map. He rents a car and drives to the pond. By then it is all silted over: there is no water to be seen, and wild grasses have grown over the wet field that once was a pond. Feeling rather foolish, Henry presses his hands to the soggy earth. Brown water bubbles around his fingers.

" 'After that,' " Henry read, " 'he could sleep with whomever he touched, for he brought utter joy to women with his hands.' "

"How flattering," said Henry. "I suppose 'V' is for Venus."

"I suppose," said Daria. "Who else gave you this gift?"

"You gave me this gift," he said. "Don't you know?" And he took her in his arms. At moments like this, Daria thought she would lose her mind loving him.

Ninety minutes later, Daria showered and left. She went back to the office and worked for a couple of hours and picked up food for the family on her way home. For once her daughter wasn't sulking, and they had civil and interesting dinner conversation.

Her affair with Henry continued for two years. Daria awoke every morning and told herself what day of the week it was and thought about how far or near it was from Tuesday. Wednesday was okay because she had just seen him, and Thursday wasn't bad either. But Friday was terrible because by then she yearned for him again, and it was still *four days till Tuesday.*

Once again, as with Pierre and the others, Daria saw how deprivation heightens joy. But she had never been as crazed as this. By the time Tuesday came and she stepped off the elevator and walked down the hall to his apartment, just pushing his doorbell made her breathe fast. He would take her straight to the bedroom and she would whimper under his touch. He would soon find out how excited she was. "Poor baby," he would say pityingly.

Once when he just flicked her and she came, he looked down on her and laughed and laughed. And for the first time in her life she came twice in a row.

"God, are you hot," he said, stroking her behind.

"Just with you."

He ran his hand between her buttocks. He did a lot of that, and more, when they were making love. When she felt his finger poking into her like a fat thermometer, sometimes she'd push his hand away. It was the only thing he did she didn't love, and still she didn't really mind and would never have stopped him if she wasn't sometimes sore there later on.

Daria's favorite single moment with Henry wasn't really sexual. They were lying on the couch, fully dressed, both facing the ceiling, just before she had to go home. His head lay under her chin, and his back was on her belly. She put her hands on his forehead, holding him to her, adjusting her breathing to his. "I'm so happy," she said.

"So am I."

Because she was married, they couldn't speak of love.

Perhaps he saw they'd reached a limit and he wanted more. Perhaps he was frightened at how dependent on her he'd grown. Perhaps he had met a wonderful new woman. Each of these hypotheses seemed plausible to Daria. It was the third year of their affair, and Henry, while still avid for her body, seemed increasingly remote.

One Tuesday when she arrived, Henry gave Daria a pat intended to appease, not arouse. He said, "We have to talk." He steered her to the living room, where the food was laid out as usual.

"What is it, Henry?" Daria asked. They didn't usually get to the food for some time.

"I don't tell you much about my other life," he said. "My life between Tuesdays."

"That's true," she said. "And Bettina certainly keeps mum."

"At my request," said Henry.

Daria sat on the couch. "Are you serious about someone? Is that it?"

Henry paused just a moment before nodding.

Daria managed to say, "Well, that's okay. I mean, I've got Lewis."

"She wants to get married," said Henry.

"Gee. What do you want?"

"I want to give it a chance. But every Tuesday afternoon there's you. And it's always so incredibly intense."

Daria nodded.

Henry continued. "Somehow, it isn't fair to Cindy."

"Cindy!" Tears sprang to Daria's eyes as she said, "What a wimpy name."

"She's not a wimp at all."

"I don't want to know about her."

"I'm sorry," said Henry. "I think we should cool it for a while."

"You mean, no more Tuesdays?"

He nodded.

"And today?"

"We'll eat, talk, drink some wine. Daria, every week when you rang the bell, I'd thank God for the hours ahead. I've loved every minute of our affair. But it couldn't last forever."

"Not forever," she said, trying to smile, "but I thought perhaps another dozen years."

He touched her neck, with the usual result. She said, "How can I stop wanting you?"

"You just will."

Daria shook her head. "I'll be longing for you for the rest of my life." She laughed to make it a joke.

He put both hands on her upper arms. "Daria—what can I do?"

"Break up with Cindy," she said promptly.

"Seriously," said Henry, stroking her arms so they seemed to flicker with warmth from within.

The trouble is, Daria thought, there's this pairing for me—Henry and ecstasy. I have to break that link.

"Henry," she said slowly, "I think you should, I mean we should—somehow you and I have to have . . . bad sex."

"What?" His fingers stopped moving on her arms.

Daria said, "Then I won't feel so sad that you're breaking up with me."

"One bad time will do it?"

"I think maybe three. Can you give me today and two more times?"

He hesitated.

She said, "Never mind about you and Cindy! You also owe something to me."

"Of course I do. But, Daria. How on earth are the two of us going to manage bad sex?"

She thought a bit and told him some things.

Henry said, "It doesn't sound like fun."

She said, "That's the point. Come on, Henry, please."

So they went to the bedroom to have some bad sex.

"No, no!" she said soon when they were on the bed naked. "You're not supposed to do the things I like!"

"But I like them too."

"Please. Not now. Remember what we're doing."

Henry cupped her breasts and asked, "Can't I even do this?"

She knew he could quietly hold them for minutes on end, varying the pressure infinitesimally while she sighed and moaned. "Have mercy," said Daria. "No foreplay. Come in."

"If you insist," he said, entering her. He began one of his slow, delicious strokes.

"Not like that!" Daria said. "Fast and hard, like a jack-hammer."

His rhythm grew fast, he shut his eyes tight. A grimace contorted his face.

She squeezed him encouragingly. Although she didn't like this staccato rhythm she'd commanded, if he didn't come soon, she just might. She touched him again, and he shuddered mightily. Then he was still. His weight was heavy upon her. He seemed to have fallen asleep. She tried to ease out from under him, but he wouldn't let her leave.

"My darling," he murmured, stroking her head. She saw it hadn't been all that bad for him.

"None of that, Henry," said Daria, slipping away from his embrace. She knew how afterplay became foreplay with him. "I have to go."

"So soon?"

"It's best." She had to leave dissatisfied. "See you next Tuesday for more."

"Are you sure about all this?" He put on his glasses and sat up in bed. His furry tits sagged.

"Oh, I am," said Daria. "It's working already."

"Hello," Henry said enthusiastically the next week. He fingered her blouse. "Nice silk."

He guided her toward the bedroom. "Remember, bad sex," she reminded him, for he was touching her neck.

"Of course."

"Could you be utterly passive today? Just lie there like some effete king?"

"I guess so. You mean, I'm not supposed to do anything?"

"Nothing at all."

"If you insist."

He lay flat on his back on the bed. She had to push his hands off her breasts when he forgot his instructions, and when she went lower, she twice removed his hands from her head. Then she moved up on his body and sat down on him hard, jamming it in. She rode vigorously up and down. She kept her eyes open and watched. She saw how he gasped at the end: "Daria, Daria, Daria!"

She was unmoved by any of it.

Daria thought about canceling their third session. After all, she was probably already free from Henry's spell. She needed only one more treatment for her cure—and it held no appeal for her at all.

As Daria sat by the phone, she vowed she would never let anything like this happen again. Never again would she sleep with an unmarried man! That would be another adultery rule. Besides, there was health to consider. Henry had tested HIV negative, he had told her, but did he *keep* getting tested? And what about Cindy?

When Daria called to break her last date with Henry, she got his answering machine. At the sound of his voice, she felt swollen below, so she realized she wasn't quite over him yet. She left no message and appeared at his door the next Tuesday as usual.

Past Henry's shoulder, she saw the small plates and bowls in the living room. She found she was very hungry, especially for some wrinkled black olives (although she knew they'd make her breath bitter). She gazed longingly at them.

But Henry was taking her into the bedroom for her final treatment. "One second," she called, breaking free from him. She scurried into the living room and prepared a plate for herself—olives, fresh mozzarella, and peppers. She sat down on the couch with it and he sat next to her. He broke some bread off a long loaf for himself and ate it dry, watching her, bemused.

"Any special instructions?" he asked. "For the bedroom?"

She nodded grimly.

"Well?" he asked.

"Try to guess."

He made a gesture and she nodded. She asked, "How did you know?"

"It's just about the only thing we haven't done—you never seemed interested. Are you ever going to finish eating?"

"I'd like another glass of wine, thank you."

Henry groaned. Daria smiled. It was fun to call the shots, and she needed the wine, and she stayed in the living room as long as she could.

Finally they went to the bedroom. Soon, she wished she were drunker. She had never loved Henry, she thought while he made love to her as if she were a boy. But unlike a boy, she had no secret pleasure spot to access through the rectum. Buggery hurt, and was ugly, and she wouldn't miss Henry one bit.

He gripped her buttocks savagely and screamed.

Moments later, he eased out of her, and soon after that he was asleep, smiling slightly, like a Buddha. She held him in her arms one final time. Then she looked at her watch and pulled away.

He opened his eyes and smiled. "What's your hurry?"

"I have to be back at two for a meeting."

He stroked her arm, and all along her nerves and muscles, her cells felt magnetized.

"Don't, Henry," she said. "It would spoil everything." She stood up near the bed.

"We have to talk," he said. "I've been thinking. Maybe we can still manage Tuesdays. At least until Cindy moves in."

"I don't think so, Henry." She thought, I couldn't do this twice.

She closed the bathroom door and had a long, hot shower, bending over to wash out her ass.

When she left the apartment, she said, "See you later," the ultimate inaccurate banality.

Bettina and Daria were having lunch at the coffee shop three weeks later. Bettina said, "*You're* doing fine. Since you and Henry broke up."

"I suppose. I devised this weird cool-down program for us. I think it really worked."

Bettina hesitated. Finally, she said, "For you, maybe—not for him."

"Oh?"

"He won't explain it, but he seems to be obsessed with you. He's still seeing Cindy—but he talks about you all the time."

Daria felt her eyes sting with tears—whether for Henry or herself she didn't know. She kept her eyes down, so Bettina wouldn't see.

Bettina said, "He can't believe you broke up with him when you did."

Daria asked, "How do you mean?"

"He said, 'Not after all that incredible sex!' "

Through her tears, Daria burst out laughing.

It was three years before Daria took another lover. He was good-looking and married, and the sex wasn't bad.

My Lover's Family

I PROWL THEIR ROOMS, STUDY THEIR books, sully the conjugal bed. He lives here with his wife and son and daughter, who inspire me with dread and fascination. The decor of the house reveals little about them, but I keep trying to learn who they are, how he fits. These three, and the others (an older sister, a dying father, a masochistic mother-in-law), form a constant backdrop to our long affair: we discuss their achievements, illnesses, and quirks afterward, in the restaurant. It is a given that we are each happily married and devoted to our families.

His mother-in-law cleans his house, although she is seventy-six. "It makes her feel useful," says my lover, "and we can't seem to stop her." I ask, "Does she have the key?" "Yes," he says, "but she doesn't just drop in. She comes to clean on Thursdays." Our day is Friday, unless one of his cohabitants, or mine, is sick or on vacation. Many people have to be well for my lover and me to have sex.

His son is fifteen. Johnny's voice is sweet and eager on the phone. I have heard it twice. He said, each time, "Hello?" I said, each time, "May I speak to Mr. Jamison, please?" (Sometimes, making love, that's what I call him, in homage to our past.) Johnny said to me the first time, "Just a moment, I'll get him," and these commonplace words made me flush.

"I think she drinks because of her husband." "Her husband?" I asked. "How do you mean?" He had been my lover, then, for only a year. "He's such a womanizer," I was told. I became aroused and angry. "That's just her excuse," I said. Neither he nor I have an open marriage; the presumption of fidelity is essential. I am not the cause of her pain. I have not driven Mrs. Jamison to drink. She's made her own choices—among them, Mr. Jamison. Or is that just *my* excuse?

His daughter is twenty. She came home unexpectedly one afternoon three years ago. Luckily, we were sitting in the living room, fully dressed, with some typed pages near us. Unluckily, the air was thick with lust and guilt and marijuana. Susan gave me an angry look. Remembering the many times her days home from school had stopped me from fucking her father, I gave her an angry look back. She went off to the kitchen and banged around with ice trays for ten minutes. I gathered the papers, returned them to my briefcase, and said, "We'll have to have another conference soon, Mr. Jamison."

When I was really his student, he didn't interest me at all. I was eighteen, he was thirty-five, quite beyond the pale.

Meeting him ten years later, the only question was where. His house is where. If we're caught, it will be by someone in his family.

He had two very good years with his son, when Johnny was thirteen and fourteen. Before that, Johnny was close with his mother, and now he is busy with his own friends. But for two years my lover was pals with his son, and now that the boy has moved on, Mr. Jamison is often sad, even with me.

Once when he was in the bathroom, I opened the large bottle of cologne that rests on his wife's dresser and touched the glass stopper to my wrists. I'd never tried the scent before, it was wonderful on me. I bought some on my way home, and now I wear it all the time—except, of course, when I visit him.

Johnny said to me the second time, "Mrs. Jamison's out." "Mr.," I said, "*Mr.* Jamison." "He's out too." "I'll call back," I said. His voice was deepening; my heart was pounding. My lover used to keep a pinup poster on the inside of his closet door, but he took it down last month: because of Johnny? He himself began with women at fifteen, but he will not describe the first occasion or female. He says, "A gentleman never tells."

His sister found a lump in her breast two years ago. A divorcee, she turned to my lover for help. Together, they consulted one doctor after another. Alone with me, he rarely smiled. He began making love without taking off all my clothes. She had surgery and radiation. She got well and went back to work. But my lover has stopped taking off my brassiere. Is he frightened of feeling a lump? Or do my breasts look better molded, bound, hidden to his eyes, forbidden? Seven years. By the third year we were into fancy stuff, and lingerie, but he would take it off.

Why doesn't a gentleman tell? Secretly, I suspect incest. A cousin? His *sister*? Why else will he not say with whom, why else shield a female or himself more than three decades after the event?

His wife has better breasts than I, or did when the picture was taken. She is topless, laughing, near a pond. The photograph is on the side wall by his desk. We have neither met nor spoken, his wife and I, yet we have the same man, on the same bed, often, no doubt, the same day. Mr. Jamison likes a lot of sex, I don't mind that he makes love with his wife. What I mind is that she drinks and that he never told me. I want to know his troubles, his joys, what his life is like. Of course, it is part of our code that we speak only well of our mates.

One night, his children hear him with his wife and the next day, at the breakfast table, they imitate his sounds. This is not the sort of thing I like to hear about his home life. "Weren't you embarrassed?" I ask, blushing at the idea. He says, "Nah—I just laughed. I said to Johnny, 'Your turn will come.'" "You didn't!"

His father, eighty-six, is in a nursing home. He's had three operations this year. "Selfish old man," says my lover. I protest, "But he looks so saintly." In a family photograph on the piano, the old man's face is fragile and benign. My lover says, "Don't be fooled. He poisoned my childhood. I could tell you stories. I wish he'd die already." "You don't mean that." "I do." "Your own *father*?" "Damn right. And stop sniveling. He's a nasty bastard." Later, in the bedroom, I cry some more. It used to unnerve him, this occasional weeping of mine during sex. Now perhaps he understands. If I breathe raggedly, he touches my cheeks to see if they're wet, he's hoping they are.

I refuse to feel guilty because of his wife. No wife can get what I get, the man at his best, his most beguiling, when he just wants to please and be pleased. I sometimes feel I even benefit his wife. After being in the bedroom with me, he's relaxed, good-natured, cordial—not his usual characteristics. His wife should be grateful. Or so I tell myself.

Last week, his wife, ostensibly accidentally, opened a letter I wrote him which began, "My darling." Confronted, he told her I was someone he'd met at a conference and would never see again. My heart ached for them both—but I wasn't pleased to hear myself described thus. "What else could I tell her?" he asked. Tell her we have a vacation each Friday. Tell her we've been doing it for years. Tell her that we do what we like best: talk and touch, drink and smoke. Tell her the truth, tell her you love me, the love of your life you once said, tell her I'm no threat at all to your family.

Piazza del Popolo

ROME WAS DIFFERENT FOR ADRIENNE this time. Then, she'd been twenty and traveling alone, indulging in the pleasures of the flesh. Now, she was thirty and touring with husband and child. Ned had never been to Rome before and he wanted to see all the sights; Jimmy was two and newly contrary. A dozen times a day he kicked and bucked and screeched. He hated the backpack that Ned had insisted on bringing instead of the stroller, so they often took taxis and often got cheated. Last time, Adrienne had been too poor to take cabs—but she'd soon met Romans with cars. It had been summer, then, stark, glaring, hot on the Piazza del Popolo. Now it was a cool and rainy spring, and men didn't speak to her on the street anymore.

But of course, she was always with husband and child. The Martins made their way down the Via del Babuino. Ned walked on steadily with Jimmy on his shoulders and his camera by his hip. Guidebook, map, and phrase book bulged the pockets of his jacket. Not very attractive, thought Adrienne—but was she any better? She held the bulky canvas backpack by its aluminum frame and carried a tote bag containing diapers, toys, and the telephoto lens. Then, she had traveled effortlessly from country to country, her summer wardrobe, light and easy (and her morals to match). Now, a morning sortie was a major expedition.

It was almost noon, and Adrienne wondered if they should get Jimmy back to the hotel so he could nap before lunch or if they should continue down the street. Already they had been to the Trevi Fountain and the Spanish Steps. If they kept on walking, they would come to the Piazza del Popolo, the only sight in Rome she wanted to see again. Last time, Adrienne's hotel had been just around the corner from the piazza, and she remembered its grandeur, its twin churches, its eerie emptiness on the August afternoons she had waited for Massimo's Alfa Romeo.

"Jimmy's going to have to walk," said Ned. "My neck's acting up again." Ned, who was thirty-seven, had a recurrent stiff neck, and Adrienne sometimes had back pains. It had recently occurred to her that already they were accruing the ailments they would carry to old age. As a twenty-year-old, she had given no thought whatever to health problems, not even sexual ones. At the time, you could get away with behavior such as hers without serious physical consequence. Adrienne had often rejoiced that it had been her lucky lot to have gone to college during the brief window of time after the birth control pill and before the advent of AIDS.

Now, married (and faithful) for the past five years, Adrienne wished she had made even greater use of her particular historical advantage. She had no regrets—except, perhaps, for the two afternoons that began at the Piazza del Popolo.

Ned placed Jimmy on the ground. "Carry-you, carry-you," Jimmy said promptly. He began tugging at Adrienne's hips.

"Not now, Jimmy," she said. "Let's walk a bit." She took one of his hands, and Ned took the other. But as soon as they started walking, Jimmy let his legs go limp so Ned and Adrienne had to haul him between them. Adrienne removed her hand from Jimmy's, and he calmly sank to the pavement. "Carry-you," he said softly.

"I'll carry you later," said Adrienne. She turned to Ned. "Perhaps we'd better go back. It's almost his nap time."

Ned sighed and shook his head. "I just hope he wakes up before the restaurants close for the afternoon." The day before, Jimmy's nap had preempted their lunch. "I wonder where the cab stand is."

The air was damp as they drove back to the hotel, and flowers were vivid everywhere. There were pots of pink azaleas all the way up the Spanish Steps and carts with blue delphiniums along the entire length of the Via Bourgognona. On the corners, street venders were selling bunches of roses and irises and gladioli. Even the daisies looked fresh and appealing—although Adrienne had never liked daisies. Their smell was rank, and their stems were weedy.

They passed the provocative lingerie store Adrienne kept meaning to investigate, and then they arrived at the hotel. The cabdriver asked for twelve hundred lire, although the meter indicated only seven hundred. Ned said, *"Non è possibile."*

The cabdriver broke into a stream of Italian well beyond their comprehension, but it was clear that he was repeating his demand. He was young and tough-looking, and Adrienne wondered what Ned would do.

"Do you have any change?" he asked her.

She opened her purse. "A few coins." She handed them to him.

Seeing this, the driver began to vociferate anew. *"Allora, mille!"* he concluded furiously, holding up ten rigidly outspread fingers. Then he said something else. It was clear he was cursing them.

"I'd have given him the thousand," muttered Ned, "but no way now." He opened the door and helped Adrienne and Jimmy out of the taxi. Then, standing on the sidewalk, Ned counted out eight hundred-lira pieces. He extended his hand.

The driver shook his head emphatically. *"Mille,"* he insisted.

The hotel doorman and several passersby were watching with interest by now, and Adrienne realized that the cabdriver was trying to make them lose face. He suddenly broke into English. "I no take less than thousand," he declared, hands waving.

Ned held out his hand again. "Sure?"

The driver spat out the window and put the car in gear. Ned shrugged. The cab lurched forward and drove away, tires squealing.

"That was amazing," said Adrienne as they rode up to their room in the narrow elevator. "He ended up with nothing!"

"His choice," said Ned. "What a bummer."

But Adrienne thought it had been the most exciting event since their arrival.

They napped when Jimmy did. They had been in Rome four days, yet their jet lag seemed to be getting worse. They lay on their backs in the darkened room. "Honey?" she whispered. "You know that lingerie shop by the hotel?"

"Uh-huh."

"I wish you'd surprise me with something from there. It would be so romantic. And they have such pretty things."

"Uh."

Ned was half asleep—or pretending to be. He always drifted off just when she was feeling chatty. Or sexy. They hadn't made love since their arrival in Rome.

It was quarter to three by the time they arrived at the restaurant. The waiters were sullen and slapped down the plates, but at least there weren't any pauses between courses. Jimmy quickly grew cranky waiting for food. Over dessert, Adrienne suggested to Ned that they separate for the afternoon, Ned taking Jimmy to a nearby park and Adrienne going shopping on the Corso. The next morning, it would be Ned's turn to go out by himself: he could visit Castel Sant'Angelo and take pictures in peace. Ned agreed to the plan, but he seemed somewhat daunted when she said goodbye a little later on the street. She stuffed a spare diaper into his pocket and walked down the Via Frattini feeling airy and free. A man in a gray suit smiled at her, and she smiled back at him and kept walking. She turned right on the Via del Corso, and there was Bugati's, just where she'd remembered from the day before.

Adrienne loved even American five-and-dimes—although they were becoming an endangered species. Nothing made her feel more prosperous than strolling down the aisles knowing that she could afford anything in the store. But foreign variety stores were even better, giving clues as to everyday life in a different land. Adrienne felt you could learn as much about a country from a five-and-dime as from a cathedral—and you could find some great bargains as well. Now she wandered from counter to counter, observing the merchandise, the salesgirls, the customers. She bought only one thing, a washcloth mitt for Jimmy, but she left the store well satisfied, as though a cultural lacuna had been filled.

Now she was free to stroll down the Corso and into some clothing shops, meandering along until she'd emerge at the Piazza del Popolo, where the Corso began. She suddenly realized that she'd engineered the whole afternoon just so she could revisit the Piazza del Popolo alone. She wondered why it suddenly meant so much to her. Had it somehow come to embody lost youth and adventure? Yet she hadn't even been happy there. Indeed, leaving Massimo's car the second time, she had felt the greatest degradation she had ever known.

The Corso was crowded with shoppers. Disappointingly, most of the clothes on display were American: jeans, overalls, sweatshirts. Last time, looking American had been gauche; now it was the latest chic. Thunder sounded in the distance. Adrienne wondered where she could buy an umbrella—another weight to add to their load. They had three large leather suitcases at the hotel, and Adrienne was already dreading their cumbersome journey to Nice.

It began to rain, and as Adrienne couldn't see anyplace to buy an umbrella, she took shelter in a small boutique. The rain smashed at the pavement outside, and Adrienne wondered if Ned and Jimmy were back at the hotel yet. Suddenly, all the lights in the shop went out. The salesgirl calmly reached for a kerosene lamp and lit it. Temporary blackouts were apparently common in Rome: this was the third since Adrienne's arrival. They lasted only a few minutes—but the downpour might last another hour. She'd have to forget about the Piazza del Popolo for the day. Adrienne smelled something heavy and unpleasant, and she turned to see a vase of daisies by the cash register. She marveled once again how anyone could like the smell of daisies.

The rain seemed to be letting up, and as she wasn't far from the hotel, she decided to make a dash for it in the lull. She thanked the salesgirl and left the shop. All the lights on the street came back on again, and she ran in the lightly falling rain until she was breathless.

*   *   *

The restaurant was very romantic: candles, roses, a strolling guitarist. They had been seated in the far corner of the room, with a buffer zone of empty tables around them, and the waiter had been dispatched for a cushion for Jimmy. (By now, Adrienne knew that no restaurant in Rome would provide either high chair or booster seat—let alone a kiddie menu.) Jimmy began throwing pieces of bread to the floor.

"No, no," said Adrienne. Ned pushed the bread basket to the other side of the table. "See, here's your book about the cat."

"No book," said Jimmy, his voice rising. "Mant bread."

Adrienne decided that the only way she could endure another restaurant meal with Jimmy was to get drunk beyond the point of caring—as she had with Massimo and Giorgio ten years earlier. Now she finished her glass of wine and poured herself another. The waiter came back with a cushion, and another waiter seated four dumpy American girls two tables away from them. Adrienne felt sorry for the girls.

The antipasto occupied Jimmy for the next few minutes: he loved cold cuts and olives. He was triumphantly waving a slice of salami around, when he knocked over his water glass. Ned threw his napkin on the table to stop the water from sliding off the edge. Adrienne calmly poured herself some more wine. Luckily, Jimmy hadn't spilled *that* yet.

There was a long wait for the pasta, and Jimmy, who had been promised noodles, began cawing, "Come moonies, come moonies," and banging his spoon on the table. The wine made Adrienne expansive and detached. She reflected that it was quite remarkable how quickly Jimmy had perfected his new persona. In a matter of days, he had changed from a sunny toddler to a cranky pest. He tossed a spoon onto the table and began flapping his arms.

"Uh-oh," said Ned.

Adrienne and Ned began moving everything out of Jimmy's reach, but they weren't fast enough. He grabbed the salt shaker and hurled it to the floor, where it shattered. Ned apologized to the waiter and Adrienne handed Jimmy her keys.

"Already?" asked Ned. Adrienne's keys always interested Jimmy, at least temporarily, so she usually let him have them only as a last resort. What would she give him next?

Two tables away, the American girls were complaining about their feet and drinking mineral water. Adrienne wondered whether they ever had any fun: they looked so plodding and dull. One of them looked especially pitiable: pink, rubbery face, fat arms, wispy hair. But maybe she had the soul of a poet.

The pasta arrived, warm and bland, and Jimmy ate purposefully for several minutes. Then, replete and bored, he put several strands of spaghetti on his head and began peering around the restaurant for approval.

The fat pink girl remarked in a carrying midwestern voice, "There's the most obnoxious little kid over there."

Adrienne felt anger rise to her face.

"A total monster," continued the girl.

Adrienne put down her wineglass, and before she could stop herself, she exclaimed loudly to Ned, "Did you hear what that fat, ugly girl over there just said?"

The girl's face became pinker still, and Adrienne instantly regretted her words. But then the girl said to her friends, "There should be a law against babies in restaurants."

And Adrienne said to Ned, "They shouldn't give passports to people like her."

Ned said, "I wish you wouldn't do this, Adrienne." Then he turned to the girl and said, "I'm sorry," but she pretended not to hear.

*   *   *

The next afternoon, Adrienne squeezed Ned's hand as they passed the lingerie store. "Remember what I said yesterday when we were napping?"

"Stop insisting, Adrienne. Let's just see what happens."

That means no, thought Adrienne, for Ned wasn't given to passionate gestures. She knew he would find one excuse or another (his meager Italian, his ignorance of European sizes) to avoid doing this one small thing which would delight her. When had they stopped trying to please each other, even if it meant some small personal discomfort?

They reached the cab stand and were motioned to the third car on line. Why the *third*? Adrienne began to feel uneasy. The driver looked like the one they hadn't paid the day before. Maybe it was his brother. As they started down the street, two empty taxis suddenly flanked their own. Adrienne grabbed Ned's hand. Maybe the word was out about them in Rome and the cabbies had planned their revenge. But the other taxis soon diverged, and the Martins arrived at the Bergmans' building without being kidnapped or mugged. For once, they weren't even cheated, and Ned gave the driver a handsome tip.

The Bergmans were their only friends in Italy. Robert, a college friend of Ned's, had been living in Rome for five years, teaching English and writing poetry. His wife, Britt, was Danish and wove tapestries. They had a little girl named Pia who was a few months younger than Jimmy, but she'd been asleep when the Martins had visited three evenings earlier. Today they were all going to visit the Colosseum, which was close to the Bergmans' apartment. Adrienne knew that Ned, who had begun to lament each passing day of their vacation, was pleased to be combining a visit with friends with the more important business of sight-seeing.

Ned walked ahead with Robert, Jimmy for once uncomplaining in the backpack, and Britt pushed Pia along in her stroller. Several cats wandered near them in the ruins.

"Hccat!" exclaimed Jimmy. "Hccat!" This month he pronounced his c's with a prolonged and guttural sound. Jimmy
bounced up and down in the backpack. "Two, fee, four, fee
hccats!"

"They feed on the rats here," said Robert.

Jimmy began to wail. "Down. I want hccat. I want down."

"Later," said Adrienne. "Soon you'll get down and play
with Pia." But so far, the children had been disappointing
in their interaction. Pia hid behind her mother if Jimmy
even looked in her direction. Adrienne thought she was a
pretty child, but glum. She hadn't smiled once. Jimmy
poked his pinwheel down in her direction and she began to
whimper.

Adrienne said, "Show the cats your pinwheel."

Jimmy held it aloft again. "Pinwee—hccats!" he sang.

"Give me the camera," Adrienne said to Ned. But by the
time she had it focused, the cats were gone and Jimmy was
pouting.

"Down," he said, "I want down." And he rapped Ned's
head with the pinwheel—so Adrienne took a picture of that.

They had reached an open corridor away from cats and
tourists, and Adrienne thought that Jimmy might as well get
down from his harness. Ned crouched over and Adrienne
extricated Jimmy's feet from the holes in the backpack.
Then she held the frame stiff while Ned disengaged his
arms. "There," she said to Jimmy. "Go play with Pia."

"Say hello to Jimmy," Britt murmured to her daughter.
She tried to help Pia out of the stroller, but Pia clung firmly
to the side bars. "Maybe later," said Britt. "She's a little
shy."

Ned took several photographs: Adrienne against the stone
tiers, Robert and Britt looking glamorous under an arch, Pia
clutching her carriage. Then Adrienne noticed that Pia was
trying to rise from her stroller, so she held the handlebar
steady to help. Pia slowly pushed herself out and took a

hesitant step toward her parents. When he saw her on her feet, Jimmy began running toward her. He held his arms wide and hurled himself joyfully against her. Pia fell to the ground, screaming. Adrienne rushed to Pia's side, but Britt was there in a moment. She picked up Pia and soothed, "There, there." Blood dripped onto Britt's handwoven shawl: Pia had cut her lip with her teeth as she fell.

"She'll be fine in a minute," said Britt. "There, there, little rabbit."

"I'm terribly sorry," said Adrienne.

"It's nothing," said Britt.

"Nothing?" Ned was suddenly beside them, furious. "Jesus, Adrienne, you were right there. You should have stopped him. You know how vicious he can be."

Vicious! Adrienne just stood there, and it was worse than in the restaurant with the fat girl.

"Bad boy!" said Ned.

Tears welled in Adrienne's eyes. She knew Jimmy hadn't pushed Pia on purpose: he had had only friendly intentions.

"Oh, *God*," said Ned. "Now you're going to start *crying*."

She stared silently back at him, keeping her eyes open wide so they would reabsorb the tears that had already formed. "Certainly not," she said at last. But she was furious. It was just like Ned to lash out in a crisis, just like him to shame her and Jimmy in front of his friends!

"Come on," said Robert. Pia was calm now, passive, settled in her stroller once again. The Bergmans started walking. "No harm done," said Robert.

Adrienne forced herself to be pleasant in front of the Bergmans, but as soon as the two families parted, she felt fury surface once more.

"Back to the hotel?" Ned asked as they crossed to street to a cab stand. "We should rest up for dinner."

"Go wherever you please," replied Adrienne. "I want to be alone."

"The *principessa* wants to be alone," Ned mocked.

"You bet I do," said Adrienne. She opened the door of a taxi and told the driver to take her to the Piazza del Popolo. "*Presto, presto,*" she urged, but Ned wasn't trying to stop her. He was just watching her from the sidewalk, looking puzzled and holding Jimmy's hand.

She turned way from them and looked ahead. As the taxi drove down the street, Adrienne remembered that she had waited for Massimo's car by the lions spouting water in the middle of the square. Suddenly, she also remembered that from a pedestal above the fountains, an ancient stone obelisk rose through the air, immense and phallic. She wondered why she had forgotten the central feature of the Piazza del Popolo. But soon she would see it all clear again.

They were about a half mile from the piazza now, and the obelisk came into view. It looked clumsy and bulky, and as the cab approached it, Adrienne realized that the obelisk was hidden by canvas and ropes. When Roman monuments needed repair, they were shrouded and secured so they wouldn't fall down. Wrapped and bound, the Flaminian obelisk, once a needle to the sky, now looked like a giant mummy. So much for seeing it clear again.

"*Dove signora?*" Even when she was alone, she was no longer called *signorina*. She told the driver to let her off by the fountain, paid him, and left the taxi.

Adrienne sat on the stone lip of the fountain and dipped her hand in the water. She looked around. It was cloudy, and the square was busy with small, darting cars. Both afternoons she had waited here last time it had been very bare and bright.

The first afternoon she'd been very elated. Massimo was one of the best-looking men she'd ever seen, and she wondered where he would take her. She had met him and his flatmate, Giorgio, the night before in a café. She'd arranged to meet Massimo at three, in the Piazza del Popolo.

Massimo was twenty minutes late, and when he arrived, Adrienne was surprised to find that Giorgio was with him. Giorgio leaned forward so she could scramble into the small backseat of the Alfa Romeo. Adrienne wondered whether Massimo was dropping Giorgio off somewhere soon, but the convertible speeded and screeched though the sleeping city without any stops.

They took her to a vineyard in Frascati, and they all drank red wine outdoors in an arbor. She began to be glad Giorgio was there: he, too, was very attractive—blond, muscular, tawny. He looked like he belonged on a Hollywood construction crew, whereas Massimo, with his pale skin, black hair, and long, slender limbs, looked like a decadent prince. Conversation was awkward, as there was no language common to them all, but Adrienne and Massimo spoke English and Adrienne and Giorgio spoke French, and after a couple of glasses of wine, they were all communicating with each other very well. Giorgio's elbow nudged her own, and Massimo's leg pressed hers under the table. When they got in the car again, she knew just where they were going, although neither of them mentioned their destination. This is the ideal time, she was thinking, to make it all come true. For her favorite fantasy had always been two handsome strangers, having their way with her, taking their turns.

Massimo kissed her in the hallway as Giorgio turned the key to their apartment. All I have to do is let it happen, thought Adrienne, and she murmured "No" on the double bed only because she felt it was expected. "Yes," replied Massimo gravely, "you must to try."

Giorgio, who spoke better French than Massimo did English, held her arms back and said, "*Mais oui, ma petite.*" Massimo stroked her hair. "*Une femme et deux hommes,*"

Giorgio continued, *"c'est la plus belle chose du monde."*

"No," she said again, without conviction.

They both began kissing her. Massimo's lips were very soft and tender: almost reverent. Giorgio's were harder, and his tongue was vigorous and impudent. She lay between them, turning first to one and then to the other. Massimo caressed her neck with the tips of his fingers; Giorgio squeezed her breasts and watched as her breath came hard. He said something to Massimo, and they both laughed.

Giorgio pulled off his shirt, revealing a hard, tan torso. *"Toi aussi,"* he told her, and when she hesitated, he pulled her shirt above her head, imprisoning her arms. Massimo held her shirt tightly while Giorgio unhooked her front-closure brassiere. *"Bella, bella,"* he murmured. Then he sat astride her and played with her breasts, lightly rolling her soft pink nipples until they were hard purple nubs. He said something else to Massimo and they laughed again. They seemed to find her very amusing.

Giorgio reached over Adrienne to undo the top button of Massimo's shirt. Massimo undid the rest of his buttons while Giorgio was stroking his chest. When Adrienne heard Giorgio's hand on Massimo's skin, she felt more aroused than ever. Somehow it was thrilling to be briefly excluded, and stiflingly sweet to think that she was just their afternoon's entertainment. She put her tongue in Massimo's ear.

When Giorgio pulled at her jeans, she suddenly sat up and shook her head. Neither of them seemed at all surprised. "You are maybe thirsty," said Massimo, getting out of bed.

She *was* rather thirsty; she looked at him gratefully as he left the room. Then she watched Giorgio take off his pants. She shook her head and said "no," which he ignored. His cock was very hard and very thick.

When Massimo returned, he, too, was naked and erect,

long and white. He had a large glass of wine in his hand. He brought the glass to her lips and tipped the wine into her mouth, so that she had to swallow quickly. "Good girl," said Massimo. "Good little girl."

Now when Giorgio pulled off her jeans, she made no resistance at all. He spread her legs and showed Massimo where her blue underpants were wet, which made them several shades deeper between her legs. She was trembling with embarrassment and shame while they spoke in Italian, presumably discussing her state of arousal. Then Giorgio pulled her panties to one side to peep at her hair. *"Une blonde naturelle,"* he murmured, petting her there. *"Très jolie."* Massimo slid her underpants down while Giorgio kept his hand on her. She opened her legs to make it easier for him. But he turned away from her and took Massimo in his arms, and the two of them kissed passionately, stroking each other's hair. Watching them, Adrienne felt tears of frustation come to her eyes.

It was Massimo who broke the embrace and turned to touch her. He tickled her pubic hair very lightly, scarcely touching the flesh beneath. Giorgio tickled her under the arms. She wriggled helplessly from one to the other and heard herself say, *"Per favore!"*

Massimo said, "You want us to stop?"

"Yes."

They both stopped tickling her.

"Bon?" asked Georgio.

"Mais . . ." she began.

"Ecco!" he said, smiling as he mounted her, moving his cock into her one centimeter at a time. But before he allowed her to come, he turned her head to face Massimo. *"Soit gentil,"* he said. *"Ouvre la bouche."*

She opened her lips obediently and Massimo thrust his cock between them and sighed.

"Pauvre petite," said Giorgio, stroking her forehead. Then

lazily, confidently, he thrust hard inside her. She clutched him and screamed.

When he came, he screamed too.

Afterward, she wanted to leave at once. She got dressed without speaking and brushed her hair so hard her head hurt. "I take you back," said Massimo. Giorgio was asleep.

They didn't talk in the car. Massimo drove rather less recklessly now that Giorgio wasn't there, but during the turns, Adrienne was still thrown from one side of the car to the other. She felt nausea building in her chest as she made out the obelisk in the distance. He pulled up beside one of the churches in the square and said, "*Ciao.*"

"Good-bye." She closed the car door behind her.

Massimo said, "We see you again tomorrow at three."

Like hell you will, she thought.

That night she dreamed she was sand. It was like being dead.

Looking back, Adrienne could see why she'd done it the first time. What continued to puzzle her now, ten years later, was why she'd returned the next day. As she waited for them once more in the Piazza del Popolo, she felt thick and passive and stupid. The sun beat down upon her, and there didn't seem much reason to do or not to do anything.

Massimo honked the horn. Giorgio was in front beside him, so she got into the backseat. They drove straight back to their apartment and took off their clothes right away. Slender, white-skinned Massimo; butch, tan Giorgio. Once again they murmured in Italian as they undressed and excited her. This time she got to see Giorgio bugger Massimo, and she found Massimo's passivity strangely arousing. She couldn't resist holding his shapely head in her hands, and stroking his silky, dark hair. When his breath got hard, she knew just what to do: she gave his mouth a pinch, twisting his lips, and he came moaning and shuddering.

"*Bella, bella*," said Giorgio with savage satisfaction. Five strokes later, he was moaning too.

Giorgio left the room and came back with a towel around his waist. She and Massimo were cuddling together, which Giorgio didn't seem to like. He turned her to him roughly and dug his nails into her buttocks. With the other hand he caressed her pussy, outside and in. Massimo dreamily stroked her breasts. Giorgio removed the towel to show her he was hard again. She brought him into her body gratefully. He gave her a few strokes and then, grinning at her disappointment, he pulled out before she could come. Instead, he turned to Massimo again, and they went down on each other, sighing and moaning. Afterward, they all got dressed. Adrienne was so swollen and aroused she could scarcely fit into her jeans. When they got to the car, Giorgio pulled her into his lap, in the front seat. As the car lurched along through the late afternoon traffic, he kept his hand, carefully motionless, snug between her legs. She kept her eyes closed, so she wouldn't know if anyone was looking into the car.

At the Piazza del Popolo, he said, "*Alors, nous voici!*" Only then did he move his hand purposefully. As soon as she began to come, he opened the door and shoved her out, so that she had to stagger on the sidewalk, bucking and shuddering, while they honked and drove away. "See you tomorrow," said Massimo.

That evening, leaving Rome early, she got on a night train for Paris.

Adrienne took out a cigarette and found a small box of matches under Jimmy's bib in her handbag. She reflected that maybe the second afternoon had been an expiation for the first: waiting for Massimo and Giorgio again, she'd known full well how desolate she'd feel later, so perhaps she'd been seeking humiliation as much as pleasure. Of

course the two had been thoroughly intermingled throughout.

Now, as she smoked her cigarette, Adrienne realized she
had come to the Piazza del Popolo today not to recall being
young and adventuresome, but to revive the anguish and
abasement she had once known—and would surely never
know again.

She threw her cigarette away. Suddenly she wanted to be
with Ned and Jimmy again. She started back along the Via
del Corso. If she kept up a good pace, she could reach the
hotel in twenty minutes.

She opened the door of their room quietly, in case Jimmy
was sleeping. Sure enough, the room was darkened. Ned
placed his finger to his lips and motioned her out to the
balcony. Jimmy turned over as they walked past him, but he
didn't wake up.

"Feeling better?" Ned asked.

She nodded. "I'm sorry I ran off like that."

"And I'm sorry I blamed you so quickly back there."

They smiled at each other.

"Where did you go?" he asked.

"To the Piazza del Popolo, where I stayed last time. But
the obelisk is all wrapped up for repairs. Everything
changes," she said.

"I bought you something," said Ned. "Let me get it."

She looked after him tenderly as he went back to the
room. How quick she had been to misjudge him! Of course
he wanted to please her! Of course he understood what
made her happy! She wondered what sort of lingerie he had
chosen for her—innocent or exotic. Of course you could
have sexual surprise within marriage!

Adrienne smelled something rank. Ned returned to the
balcony with a big bunch of daisies in his hand. He gave
them to her with a loving smile.

Birthday Party

I ALMOST FORGET THE WINE. I LOOK AT my watch. I can just about get there and back in time—but I don't know if the liquor store is even open at 10:15 A.M. I put on my jacket and leave the apartment.

I pace as I wait for the elevator. A minute passes, and another—at a time when every second counts. We have each promised not to be late. Finally, I take the stairs. Downstairs, in the lobby, an old woman is energetically approaching me. "Mr. Williams?" she says hoarsely. "Ellory Williams?"

I nod. It's Mrs. Epstein from the building. She is very short, with bushy gray hair. She grabs my upper arm with surprising strength. "Mr. Williams, we're having a tenants' meeting tomorrow at eight in my apartment."

"Yes, yes," I say. For the past week, I have seen the notices in the elevator and above the mailboxes.

"Will you be there?"

"I'll certainly try. And now, if you'll excuse me . . ." I give my arm a little shake, but she has her talons curled around my sleeve.

"We'd like to count on you," she rasps. "Ah, Mrs. Green!" She crosses the lobby to shanghai another prospect—and I sprint out the door.

It's a dazzlingly bright autumn morning. People on the street are smiling, and yes, the liquor store is open.

I take a bottle of white wine to the cash register.

A beggar stops me as I leave the store, and I give him some change and hurry home.

Old Mrs. Epstein is still on the prowl, but I make it across the lobby without attracting her attention. I am back in my apartment by 10:27. There is just time to open the bottle; Vivian and I synchronized our watches yesterday.

"You really want to do this?" she said.

"Damn right I do. You?"

"Well, sure. You're the birthday boy, aren't you?

"Not the right phrase for a man of my years."

"Thirty-eight's not senile," she said fondly.

"By comparison with you . . ." I replied.

I'm fifteen years older than Vivian, a source of much excitement to us both. I like to show her new things, I like to hear how she likes them. In bed, she's tender, ardent, orally inclined. Heavenly. There's only one way I would like her to change.

It's 10:29. I press down the chrome arms of the air-pressure corkscrew she gave me. The cork comes out cleanly, with a satisfying thwock. The next half hour will be something new for both of us.

I gave him the corkscrew because his cunning-looking antique one—a curlicue of black iron set in a three-knuckle handle—demanded too much effort and finesse. He looked at the new corkscrew warily. "Don't be such an old bachelor," I said, pulling his mustache. "Come into the twentieth century."

He said, "I might as well try it out now." He got a bottle of wine from the refrigerator. He carefully applied the new tool. The cork came out steadily, smoothly, easily. "Nice," he said, "I must admit." He poured us each a glass of wine.

I meant to tell him then. But we sipped, we looked at each other, we put down our glasses, and moved closer. So it wasn't until the next morning that I said, "I'm leaving the city next month. On a tour."

"Congratulations." His voice was not enthusiastic. "How long?"

"Six weeks. Small cities upstate." I'd been with Calabash, a new dance company, for almost a year, and these were our first out-of-town performances. The engagement was sudden: we were filling in for a more famous troupe. "I've got the solo in 'Parallax,' " I told Ellory.

"Terrific," he said gloomily.

I was sad too. We'd met three months before, at a street fair, and now we were very much in love. He often told me how lucky he was, but I thought I was the lucky one. I'd never met a man like him—cool-witted, warmhearted, hot-blooded.

Ellory gave a sigh. "I just realized," he said, "you'll be away for my birthday."

These are some things Vivian tried for the first time with me: artichokes, satin sheets, Roland Barthes, hockey games, papayas, racquetball, meditation, Amaretto, and dirty words in bed.

Did I happen to mention her mouth, her small, exciting mouth? Girlish, pouty lips, shaping the most lubricious phrases, many of her own devising.

I also introduced her to erotic lingerie. Today, she has promised, she'll be wearing her blue satin tap pants, cut wide enough in the leg for easy access. She wants me to be wearing only a shirt with cuff links.

"Cuff links, Vivian?"

"Yes. Fastened. The shirt, though, should be unbuttoned. The whole effect should be one of impetuous haste."

I said, "Don't be late."

"I'll be ready. I promise. Oh, and, Ellory . . ."

"Yes?"

"I know you don't believe in paranormal phenomena, but let's really try to be together. You with me all the way."

"You with me too," I said. Vivian once confided to me that when making love, she has to fantasize to come. After that, I sometimes tried to make her look at me, think of me. It didn't work: she had to close her eyes and ride alone to get there. "You've been a slave to those fantasies for years," I said. "Perhaps this new way you'll have some sort of breakthrough."

Panties. The very word sounds naughty. Since I've known Ellory, I've bought a dozen pairs of panties, he appreciates them so. "Ah," he murmurs, his mustache brushing my belly. "I see you've been shopping. I must investigate." The examination is thorough: fit and fabric are carefully assessed. He likes the blue satin tap pants the best, because he can get in me right through them, he must like the soft fluid feel of the fabric against him.

On his birthday, I'm wearing his favorite panties, as promised, and a white silk camisole. I shiver. Although it's a beautiful bright autumn day, the hotel room is chilly. I wrap a cashmere shawl around me and return to the green flowered sheets.

One time, at dawn, he said, "Do you ever touch yourself?"

"Of course—doesn't everyone?"

"Show me," he said.

"Now?"

"Yes."

Somehow I couldn't. "You do it to yourself," I said.

"Okay."

I watched for a few minutes, fascinated and aroused. "That's terrific," I said.

"Now you."

"I can't."

"Vivian, that's not fair."

"You're right," I said, "but I can't." One reason I agreed to this birthday party was that I felt guilty about that other time. Now it's 10:30 exactly. For once I am ready on time. Oh my darling.

At first I thought we'd use the telephone for this. But Vivian said there was no direct line to her room. Understandably, she doesn't want a telephone operator eavesdropping on our conversation. So it has to be silent communion this day, an assignation of the minds and hands while we are still apart. We are to think of each other, picture each other throughout. And perhaps this long-distance rendezvous will help liberate Vivian from her fantasies. After all, she'll be thinking of me, and not the anonymous truck drivers and decadent playboys who usually people her fantasies.

It seems that men, for excitement, picture particular women, individuals they know, in erotic situations. Women's fantasies, however, usually involve faceless strangers in exotic and unchanging scenarios. But I want her to think of me. I want to crash her private party. Today, hundreds of miles from Vivian, I want to be really with her when she comes.

I put down my wineglass and unbutton my shirt. I picture her entering my apartment, closing the front door behind her. She is taking off her pink beret and shaking out her black, spiky hair. She is pulling her hair up and out while her nipples rise under her sweater. She is licking her bottom lip, smiling. She is asking me if I like her perfume. She is putting her fingers under her skirt, then holding them under my nose. I am pushing her down on the bed, raising that skirt, caressing those blue satin tap pants.

The telephone rings, and I smile as I lift the receiver. "Hello, Ellory," I say. "If you're calling to check, I'm all set."

"All set for what?" asks my mother. "Vivian, I have to talk to you."

"Mom—hi! How on earth did you find me?"

"It was no easy matter, my love. First I called the theater where you performed last week, then they told me you'd be in Utica today, then I called the . . ." She goes on like this a while.

"Mom? Is there any particular reason you went to all this trouble tracking me down?" I look at my watch; now Ellory has a good head start. Or hand start.

"Well, darling," says my mother. "I wanted to hear your voice. I wanted to know what you were doing at this very moment."

"At this very moment, I'm talking to *you*," I say crossly. Then I have to laugh.

"What's so funny?"

At this very moment, Mom, I'm breaking a masturbation date with my lover. "Nothing much," I say, giggling. "At this very moment, I'm wearing the cashmere shawl you gave me for Christmas and speaking to you from my bed."

"All set for what?" she asks shrewdly. "What were you going to tell Ellory?"

"I, um, it's his birthday, I'm just getting set to write him a letter telling him how I feel about him." I picture him on his bed, in the shirt with the cuff links, with a wineglass nearby.

"Don't tell him everything," she warns. My mother is of

the old school of feminine wiles and is constantly urging me to hold back and retain my "aura of mystery."

"*Mother*," I say, "not this again. How's Dad? And Sylvia?"

"They're fine."

"Good. Well, then . . ." I make no attempt to keep the impatience from my voice. I look at my digital watch: 10:38 changes to 10:39, and I'm breaking my promise to Ellory.

"Vivian," says my mother, "I heard from Robert Lewis again."

"Oh, Mother, *no*."

I am panting as I caress those blue satin tap pants. I open my eyes and glance at the clock. I'm getting too excited too fast—it's only 10:39! I cross my arms behind my head. I rest a minute. Then I get up and refill my wineglass. I go back to bed. This time I begin thinking not just of Vivian but of what she's told me she thinks of during sex. I ease myself into one of her fantasies and decide to stay with it awhile. It might slow me down and also, perhaps, lead to the quasimystical communion for which she yearns. I yearn, of course, for a breakthrough: Vivian thinking, while coming, of me. I put down the glass to begin again.

Sssss. The air brakes hiss as I pull my tractor-trailer to the side of the highway. I lean my head out the window and back up fifty feet along the shoulder to where Vivian stands in her red miniskirt and her black leather jacket, shivering in the wind. She doesn't even ask how far I'm going, just hops up into the cab and blows on her fingers. I pat her thigh through her skirt. "You'll be warm in a minute," I say. I do not start the truck. I keep patting and stroking her thigh. "Please don't," she says. But her leg is willing in my hand. "Not even up here?" I say, going higher. She does nothing to prevent my progress upward. "My goodness," I say. "You're all ready and willing." She moans. I chuckle. I lift up her skirt. I pull her panties aside. "What a cutie," I say as I play there. "My buddies are going to go wild for this." She is shuddering helplessly in my hand. I give her crotch a lazy tickle—but wait! This is the wrong fantasy! How can I be driving a truck if I'm wearing cuff links?

Robert Lewis is a young lunatic I knew five years ago. I do not use the word "lunatic" lightly. During our one and only date, he told me I was like Circe, Ariadne, Scarlett O'Hara, and Petunia Pig. He said, "God, you're so beautiful and yet—" His voice broke. His hands trembled. It's one thing to paint scenery with an admiring if deranged young man, but quite another to be his date for the evening. I made excuses for the next week or so, then summer stock was over and I was living at home again, majoring in dance at the university nearby. When Robert called, I told him it would never work between us. I wished him the best, but there was no point in our seeing each other. After his third emotional and threatening phone call, I told my mother to screen my calls and tell him I was away. This she did, and Robert Lewis developed a hatred for her as irrational as his passion for me. After a month, he sent me an ivory necklace—which I immediately returned. Then he left a package on the front step for my mother. She opened the wrapping to find a large pickle jar. There, floating in the water, was what could only be one of his feces.

That winter, Robert's parents committed him to an asylum, and we heard no more from him. "What did Robert have to say?" I ask, unnerved to know that he is on the scene again.

"Now, this was all last week, so I don't want you to worry, but I think you should know."

"What, Mom, what?" Wait, Ellory, wait!

"Robert wrote me a note in these crazy hodgepodge letters, saying he'd never forgive me and he was going to get me. And I wasn't really worried till the part about the gun."

The gun? The time! It's 10:45—yet I can't end this conversation. "What do you mean?"

"He said he had a gun and he was going to use it. It turns
out he was off lithium. You see, the next day I spoke to his
mother, and she said . . ."

Her voice goes on. Right now, Ellory is thinking of my
breasts, of my skin, of my collaboration in this birthday
party—hoping I'll break through. Yet here I am, trapped on
the phone. I try to cut into my mother's flow with a sum-
marizing statement, so I can say good-bye and get in on the
finale with Ellory. "So, Mom, Robert's back on the drug now
and in the sanitarium again?"

"Yes. I must say, it's quite a relief. And it's also a relief
about those hospital tests. . . ."

"Tests!" I yelp. "You never told me you were taking any
tests!"

If I am wearing cuff links, we are at a château in the
Loire. Vivian has described this scene to me in detail. I am
the marquis, she is the chambermaid. For weeks I've been
taking liberties with her—stroking her neck, feeling her
breasts. Usually, I get her good and excited, then give her
ass a slap and say, "Now run along, you tempting minx!"
Today she appears in my room, with her feather duster, as
I am getting ready for dinner. "Excuse me, sir," she says,
brushing by me. I allow her to pass unpetted, but as she
begins to dust the top of a corner closet, I slip my hand under her skirt and begin fondling her bottom. She kind of
settles into my hands. I just keep teasing her. "I bet you
want it today." I put my hand into her. "I know you want
it today."

Vivian wants it today. She is lying in bed in a small hotel
in Utica, New York. She is touching herself and thinking of
me, Ellory Williams, art professor and marquis. She is
moaning at this very minute.

"The trouble is," I tell her as she drops her feather duster and embraces me, "I'm rather late for dinner. I have only a minute." I carry her to the bed and spread her legs. "Is that all right with you?"

"Whatever you say, sir," she murmurs.

I open my pants and press myself into her.

And suddenly, I am there with her. There's no other way to describe it—I'm in that bed with Vivian in Utica, New York, in the white sheets, thrusting myself into my darling. She quivers, I shudder, we are there. Perhaps I scream. Perhaps I whisper Dear God.

My mother says, "Vivian, I don't like to trouble you about my health until I know I'm all right. I don't want you to worry."

"Mother," I shriek, "can't you see how this way it's worse? Now I'll worry about you all the time! What kind of tests anyway?"

"Allergy tests. You know how every fall I start sneezing and wheezing?"

"Ma, that's because of Verushka. Just get rid of that wretched cat . . ." We've covered this ground before. I picture Ellory, extended diagonally on the bed. His eyes are closed, and I am frantic to join him. "Mother," I say, "this call must be costing you a fortune."

She replies, "Don't you give two hoots about your mother's health?"

"I didn't know they gave allergy tests at the hospital."

"Hospital, medical center . . . what's the difference? It was frightening."

"What were you frightened of? Hay fever? Pink eye?"

"I was frightened that I was allergic to wheat. Imagine life without bread and croissants!"

"Mother, I have a rehearsal. I'm already late. I'm glad you don't have to live in a world without wheat. Tell me the upshot, then I'm saying good-bye. What were the test results?"

"Well, you were right—I'm allergic to cats . . . well, not really to cats, but to their dander. And every fall, when Verushka starts staying indoors, I have a histamine reaction. But how can I possibly give away my dear old Verushka? She's been with me so long. . . ."

When I finally manage to say good-bye, it's 11:02. I replace the receiver and glare at the dial. As if in response, the telephone rings again. It's Ellory, of course—breathless, laughing, happy.

I say, "Hello, my cheeky chambermaid."

"Happy birthday, sweetheart."

"God, that was great. I felt so close to you."

She makes a little noise, which can only be a purr of satisfaction. I'm so glad I thought of this celebration. I tell Vivian how I got into her fantasies and how at the end I felt I had joined her, telepathically, in her white sheets upstate. I ask, "Did you think about me?"

"Of course."

"The whole time?"

"I promise you, Ellory." There is no mistaking the truth in her voice, yet she sounds inexplicably rueful. "I thought about you the whole time."

"That's terrific," I say. No more anonymous truckers or nobles—I am her fantasy now! "What a breakthrough—on my birthday! It's the best present you could ever give me! Don't you think? Vivian? Darling?"

Final Assignment

1.

"Hello, Kyra."
"Hello, Philip."
"Here we are."
"Uh-huh."
"Together at last!"
"Mm."
"You're so lovely! I always knew we'd be incredible together. What's so funny?"
"Nothing."
"Tell me. I want to know."
"Now?"
"Yes."
"Well—you talk so much!"
"You're very talkative yourself."
"Yes, but not . . ."
". . . while doing this?"

"Right."

"Well, this the happiest way I converse."

"Really?"

"Oh, yes. My favorite mode of intercourse. Talk to me, Kyra."

"I'll try. But it's hard."

"Hard things can be very rewarding."

"Indeed."

"So, how is it?"

"It's strange, Philip."

"Is it nice?"

"Yeah."

"Tell me more."

"I can't."

"Yes, you can."

"No."

"Yes, Kyra, I want to hear it."

"Yes, then. Yes, YES."

"That's a good girl. That's a good start."

2.

"So soon? You're kidding."

"This is just a little joke."

"A *big* joke, Philip."

"It's all your fault. You're just so arousing. Now, why don't you get on top of me. Like this. Yes."

"Oh. Oh!"

"You like it this way too?"

"Yeah. This is great."

"You're just wonderful."

"You too. And I never even guessed! Despite the gossip. I never even thought of you this way."

"Really? Why not? Explain. Elucidate."

"At this very moment?"

"Of course. Just . . . keep on moving . . ."

"Well . . ."

"Go on, Kyra."

"You seemed sort of ordinary. Kind, mild-mannered. Hey! You're hurting me!"

"Take it back about mild."

"I take it back!"

"Then I'll go easy."

"It's okay. It's fine now. Oh, so fine!"

"You used to wear torn jeans."

"How can you think about that now?

"Because I thought about this then—when you sat in front and I could see into those jeans."

"And I in all innocence simply took notes."

"All innocence indeed. You sat in front. You wore those tight T-shirts. You got your A."

"Sexist pig! I *earned* my A! It was easy. I was smart."

"And smug."

"Only about school."

"And now?"

"Everything's harder without grades."

"Do you want to be graded?"

"Do you?"

"Just a short evaluation, baby. Twenty-five words or less. Now. Right NOW."

"Oh, Philip. Beyond words."

3.

"Nothing's really beyond words."

"The English teacher's credo! God, it's been a week. Do you always take up where you left off?"

"It's a useful talent in my line of work."

"Am I still your old student?"

"Sometimes. Could you put your hand in back of . . ."

"Right here?"

"Yeah! Great!"

"Because I think of you a lot as my old teacher."

"Don't say that."

"Of course not, *old*. I meant former. I've never known anyone so young."

"You mean this?"

"Yes. That vigor. And the way you curve up to watch as if in disbelief."

"Don't you watch?"

"No. Usually my eyes are closed."

"Not with me."

"No, because, Philip, it's . . ."

"What?"

"God, I love it like this, just like THIS."

"You mean with your clothes on because I couldn't wait to get at you?"

"Oh! Oh!"

"Baby, turn over. Careful. Well done."

"Go on, then. Go."

"HERE. Take it all."

4.

"Easy."

"Sorry. You're so delicate, I forget."

"And you're so big, no one would guess, it's so funny."

"I've been thinking of doing this with you all week."

"And I've been thinking of you."

"What I like so much is the way you turn all pink and—"

"Philip, what was that noise?"

"Just the people upstairs."

"Are you sure?"

"Kyra, relax. Nobody's going to walk in on us."

"No chance that your wife—"

"It's very unlikely. Anyway, it would be my problem, not yours."

"I guess."

"Relax. Take it easy."

"I'm sure you've done this lots before, but it's kind of scary for me."

"We can't always go to hotels. I can't afford it! But what about your place?"

"Out of the question!"

"Well, then. You don't want us to stop doing this?"

"Oh, no."

"Are you sure?"

"How can you ask?"

"Tell me more."

"Philip, when I said I loved it last time, I didn't mean about my clothes, I meant with my eyes open, seeing you with me, seeing YOU."

"There, there. Oh, yeah."

5.

"Ah."

"Yes."

"Now we can talk again, Philip. Really talk."

"Okay."

"You've created this great new pairing for me. This new coupling."

"What a witty young mistress."

"That's nice like that."

"Yes, isn't it? Do you know all the things I want to do to you?"

"But face-to-face is best because we can talk."

"I see I've made a convert."

"Is what we say in bed truer than what we say normally?"

"Perhaps."

"Could you lie to me now?"

"Of course not. You can trust me."

"Can I really? I'm getting scared."

"Don't be scared. It's so nice. Hey, I've been wondering. When you came to my reading that night, did you just want me to take you to bed?"

" 'Just'? God, I feel so insulted!"

"Not 'just.' But did you?"

"No! Jesus. I was curious. It was funny to see your name after five years! And poems by people I know are always more compelling."

"And when we had lunch the next day?"

"I thought you were nice but too eager. I felt so in control. So young yet so wise. So attractive! Was I mean?"

"Very."

"But I called the next day to apologize. Have I made amends yet, Philip?"

"Yes, but are you sorry?"

"No, I'm not sorry a bit."

"Then you deserve it, Kyra."

"What?"

"This!"

"You're hurting my hands!"

"I know."

"Oh, God! Yes. Yes!"

"All right?"

"Oh! YES . . . Thank you."

"Love."

6.

"Love?"

"Now you're doing it."

"You've taught me so much!"

"Is all this educational?"

"Yes. But don't try to divert me. You didn't answer my question."

"Perhaps I didn't hear it. I should *hope* I'm diverting you, Kyra."

"Do you know what I see when I look out this window from your bed?"

"No, what?"

"I see that blinking sign for Ryan's Bar. It's so damned ironic."

"You don't have to look."

"Perhaps I do."

"You're in a funny mood today."

"Yes. What am I doing here anyway?"

"Do you want me to tell you?"

"Okay."

"Sure?"

"Yes, tell me."

"You're cheating. Deceiving your boyfriend. Sneaking out once a week to get laid by a married man old enough to be your father."

"I can't help it, Philip. I'm crazy for you."

"Yeah? Well, you're just a slut. Shall I go on?"

"No—no—please!"

"Okay."

"Hey—*Philip*, what are you doing?"

"You told me to stop."

"I didn't mean you should actually leave—"

"Beg and I might let you have it again."

"Please. Oh, please!"

"Let me see how you're doing."

"Ohhh."

"Why, you sweet little gusher! You need it so bad . . ."

"Oh, God. PLEASE."

"Oh, all right. There you are."

"Ahhhh . . ."

"How'zit feel, bitch?'

"Fabulous. Wonderful!"

"What do you say?"

"Thank you. Oh, thank you so much."

"Look at you, wriggling and moaning! My plaything. My sex slave. My helpless young ho!"

"Oh! Oh! OH!"

"Having fun?"

"My God. I can't help it!"

"You don't know what you want, do you?"

"Do you?"

"Uh-huh. I have a great idea for next week."

7.

"Professor Nolan?

"Yes, Kyra?"

"My head's pressed against the bookshelf. . . ."

"There. Better?"

"Doesn't anyone else have the key here? Not even the chairman?"

"No, I told you. Just the custodian, and he's gone for the day. I bet he'd like to see this though."

"Don't."

"Why not? Don't stop, go on. My standards are very exacting, young lady, and I'm a very busy man."

"Professor Nolan, I'm trying my best. You're my favorite teacher, and I've worked so hard for your class."

"There, there, don't be upset, perhaps you'll get a good grade after all. You're doing very well now, really superbly for someone so young and so dumb."

"No. NO."

"Yes, you are, you just can't help yourself, can you?"

" . . . "

"I love them young and ignorant like you."

"No, not again, no."

"Oh, yes. Just like that. How old did you say you were?"

". . . They tell me I'm precocious. . . ."

"I'll say you are, little girl. My, oh my. My."

8.

"Philip, what can we do after that?"

"I know. My bedroom seems very prosaic after last week."

"At least there's a pillow for my head."

"Speaking of pillows, let me just bring it down under your . . ."

"No—not that."

"Whyever not?"

"Ryan and I sometimes . . ."

"So?"

"Look, I can't help it, I'd feel funny."

"Okay. Hey, have you cut your hair?"

"Just a trim. You're so observant!"

"It looks great but it feels a little stiff."

"Is that so? I'll have to use a conditioner there."

"Good idea. Get all soft for me."

"I already am. Philip, could you go over the classic/romantic dichotomy again?"

"Now?"

"Of course now."

"Kyra, Kyra. Oh."

"Gosh, already. What about me?"

"Hush now. Later. I promise, you'll be fine."

9.

"Have you had a good week?"

"It's been *two* weeks, Philip."

"Yes, of course."

"Anyway, no. I've been sad."

"Kyra, why?"

"I feel so bleak. I think of you so much."

"Yes, well. Just move your legs. . . . Yes, up over me like that."

"I think of you all day. I dream of you at night. I wake up talking in my sleep, about to say your name. And you're getting bored with me."

"No."

"Yes, I can tell. You've had lots of students, ex-students, colleagues . . ."

"Stop that, Kyra."

"You feel it's time to move on."

"Let's just be quiet today."

"I can't be quiet. I'm caught in the pattern."

"Shhhh."

"I just keep thinking of you."

"Well, try to stop. Oh. Come on, girl, come with me."

"Philip, I don't think I can."

"Of course you can."

"I don't think so."

"Hey, don't cry."

"I'm sorry."

"Baby. Silly. There."

"Have you ever fucked somebody crying before?"

"Yes, as a matter of fact."

"Can't I bring you *any*thing new?"

"Shhhh."

"Go on without me."

"No."

"But I can't."

"Want to bet?"

"I guess . . . not."

"You guess . . . not! Look at you. Look!"

"Yes, but this doesn't mean anything."

"Shhhh."
"Not to you I mean. Not to YOU."
"Shhhh. Easy. THERE."

10.

"I've always been curious. Do you have to do this every day?"
"So it seems."
"It's amazing. And at your great age too."
"It's a habit."
"Is that why you have to have lots of women?"
"I never said that."
"Word gets around."
"Don't let it bother you."
"I can't help it! I haven't seen you for a *month*."
"Hey, don't cry."
"Is this our last time?"
". . ."
"But what happened, Philip? I liked you so much. Was that my mistake? Getting obsessive? And showing it?"
"Shhhh. Just be quiet."
"But I have to talk! I must hear your voice! Please! Say something."
"Hush, Kyra."
"I used to wish we could take a really long car trip together just so I could hear you talk. I know you mainly liked my ass, but with me, it was your sexy mind—your hot words—your deep voice—and especially talking together like this."
". . ."
"Do you have somebody new? Is that it?"
". . ."
"Why don't you have time for me anymore?"
". . ."

"Philip, you got me talking, you have to reply. Say something. Anything! Please. Talk to me. Talk to me! Talk!"

The End

Kyra—

Don't know how to evaluate this curious ms. As fiction, it lacks texture. As drama, it lacks event. As pornography, it has too little physicality—and too much emotion.

And although many of your guesses are uncannily correct, the plot (such as it is) lacks plausibility. Why must we wait five years to begin? And I find your ending unduly despairing. Despite current convention, every good story needn't end badly.

Come to my office this afternoon. It should be fun to work on this together.

PN

The February Fantasy

I SOMETIMES WONDER WHAT IT MUST BE like, encountering Jenny that way. I picture them sitting in class that first day, waiting for the teacher to arrive. They are sixteen and seventeen and the desks are a little too small for many of them, so they fidget as they wait. The bell rings, impatience grows. Then the door opens and in comes Jenny in one of her sweaters. She's blond, twenty-three, thirty-six-twenty-two-thirty-five. "Hello," she says, "I'm Mrs. Larabee."

I'm Mr. Larabee—Paul—and when I was in high school there was a Miss Warren who taught French and who occasioned many coarse jokes about French culture. When Miss Warren wrote high on the blackboard, her dress would lift—and so would I. I almost failed French that term.

Jenny's students, however, thrive in her class. They write wonderful things about their lives and the books they are reading. Jenny loves her job and can chatter on by the hour about her students and their projects. Once, in the dark, shortly after making love, she whispered, "Paul? I've thought of the perfect way to teach metaphor."

She must be a pretty good teacher, all right—yet why must she dress that way for school?

"What way?" she says.

"Those sweaters."

"Paul, if I wear looser clothes, they just fall from my bust and make me look heavy. So I have to wear things that cling. With a body like mine, you can either look sexy or fat, and I'd rather look sexy. It's better for teaching."

"What?"

"Whenever I sense any boredom, I simply walk across the room." She smiles. I want to twist her arm. Instead, we fuck on the carpet.

"Don't be jealous of my students," she says. "You know I prefer older men. A guy isn't attractive to me unless he's at least twenty-nine."

Which is my age. I am at once dismayed at being already classified an "older man" and reassured once more that those teenagers she tantalizes pose no threat. For it seems to be true: at parties, she generally gravitates toward men of thirty-five and forty. Still, after two years of marriage, I get bothered thinking of her up at that blackboard arousing teenage lust.

"Look at this," she says with a grin after dinner one night. She hands me a composition by a Ricky Weldon, who has terrible handwriting. The class has been reading "The Secret Life of Walter Mitty," and Jenny has asked them to blend reality and daydream as Thurber did. Ricky Weldon has begun his story in a classroom. My heart sinks as I read through his scrawl.

It was the first day of school. I sat at my desk and wondered what English would be like this term. I took out my notebook and pen. I hoped I wouldn't have another teacher like Miss X last year, who had warts and recorded marks for penmanship and punctuality. The bell rang, the door opened, and my teacher walked in. And I knew I would enjoy English very much this term. She was gorgeous—blue-eyed, blond, and busty. She told us her name and what we would be doing. I couldn't stop looking at her.

Here there is a dotted line across the page, and the words "fantasy starts" in parenthesis. (Has Jenny asked them to do this?)

The teacher smiled at me as she spoke to the class, and when the bell rang, she told me to stay. She asked if I had any suggestions about English or anything. I thought of several suggestions, but only smiled back at her. She said, "Why don't we discuss it at my place?"

She drove us to her deserted home and said, "Wait here, I'll get us some coffee."

When she returned to the living room with the tray, she was wearing a loose white robe. I could see her beautiful body through it. She put down the tray and sat down very close to me on the couch. I said, "Let's forget about the coffee!"

I put down the story. "Do you often get this sort of thing?" I ask Jenny.

"Once in a while. Not usually as well written as this one. What did you think of it?"

"It's all right," I say at last, not wanting to reveal how much that used to be my fantasy—and how much it's now my fear. "I wonder what happens next?"

"Anything you want," she replies. A slow smile crosses her

face. She reaches in back of her to get a pencil and pad. She hands them to me.

"What?"

"You finish it," she tells me.

"Aw, Jenny."

"Come on, don't be stuffy. I'm not going to mark it, you know."

She picks up a magazine and starts to read. I'm annoyed—I don't much like games. But then I think of Miss Warren, and Ricky, and being sixteen and horny all the time, and I start to write.

> She pushed the table away from us and leaned against my arm. She played with my arm and my hand; she unzipped my pants and played with my cock. "Oh, let me," she said, and soon she was kissing it, licking it, sucking it. Her robe fell open, and I stroked her splendid breasts. She groaned. "Now," she pleaded, and moved up on my body. She guided my cock into her hot, ready cunt.

I'm surprised at how fast the words are coming. I pause. Jenny is reading over my shoulder. "Oh, wow," she says. "That's great. Hey—let's."

"What?"

"Wait here, I'll get us some coffee," she replies. And she goes to the kitchen, swaying her hips. I light a cigarette. Jenny is so childish at times. Still, it may be fun. We've been lovers four years, and sex beween Jenny and me has become comfortable and routine.

Ten minutes later, she is back in the room with the tray. The coffee is freshly perked; I admire her attention to detail. She doesn't have a white robe, so she's wearing her blue one, loosely tied. I see a flash of pubic curls as she sits down beside me.

"Let's forget about the coffee," I say. And then it all happens as I wrote it, and I come so hard, I bruise her shoulders with my hands.

She says, "Oh, yes."

Afterward, when we're drinking the coffee and I'm watching Jenny with a new appreciation of the people she can be, I say, "Thank you, Ricky Weldon."

She smiles. "Now I'll have to write one for you," she says.

"Not *now*, I hope."

"Of course not." She stirs her coffee and adds pompously, "The exotic should always be rationed."

So it's not for several weeks that we play Fantasy Come True again. It's a rainy Saturday night and the VCR is broken and we have nothing much to do. After dinner Jenny hands me a piece of paper. I unfold it and read what Jenny has typed:

> You are my master, I am your slave. You tie me to the bed. You caress me contemptuously; you insult me tenderly. You stroke my hair as you push your cock into my mouth. You let me suck you awhile, then you pull it out and put it in my cunt. I cannot move my hands to prevent or encourage you.

"You continue to surprise me," I say.

She blushes. "Well?"

I make my voice harsh and indifferent. "Well, what are you waiting for? Get into the bedroom where you belong and take off your clothes."

She starts down the hall, then turns to look back at me. I wave her away. "I'll be there when I'm ready. Just lie down and wait."

She leaves. I light a cigarette and consider my role—and my part. I've already got a semi from her meek obedience.

Now, what shall I tie her with? What we need is some clothesline, but I can find only a ball of string. I decide to use a few belts. Luckily, we have a four-poster, so it should be easy. (Did this occur to Jenny when we bought it?) I open the bedroom door. She's lying on her back, naked for me on the sheets.

"That's better," I say. I sit down on the bed and put my hand in her mouth and let her suck it for a while. Then I stand up again. I open the closet door and take out a few narrow leather belts, some mine and some Jenny's.

I say, "These will do. Hold out your hand." I put one of my belts around her wrist and pull it tight, like a watchband, before tying the other end to the bedpost. I always knew boy scout camp would be good for something! Efficiently, I bind her other arm. I say, "Try to move."

She can't.

"Now the legs."

"Legs? I didn't say anything about legs."

"Who's in charge here, anyway?"

I cup her breast. She is silent, but her nipple is eloquently erect in my hand. I use her belts, which are shorter than mine, on her legs, as it is closer from the bedposts to her ankles than to her wrists. I survey my work. "There! All bound and ready. You *are* ready, aren't you?" I investigate. "Whoa! You're soaking!"

I work her up a little more. I can't tell if she's straining toward me or away from me, but she can't move very much anyway because of her restraints. It is curiously exciting to touch someone who can't stop you.

I leave her panting on the bed and go to my dresser drawer. Then I return to the bed and slide my hand inside her all too easily. "This is ridiculous," I say. I start drying her off with a handkerchief, but she finds even that is exciting. I have to laugh. "Gee," I say, "it's hard to dry you off without making you even wetter!" The handkerchief is sopping.

I depart from her script to try a little experiment. She is so ripe, so ready . . . I shift my attention northward. I start sucking one of her breasts very rhythmically while I pull on the other. Sure enough! She gasps and shudders. I've made her come just by fooling with her breasts.

Her pussy is empty and ignored—but not for long. I take pity on her, and push my cock into her, crooning, "Come again for me, little ho!" At once, like an obedient love slave, she has another orgasm around my shaft, quaking and moaning so I quite lose control.

Within minutes, however, I've regained my composure, and my hard-on, and I treat her sternly and badly for another two hours.

When I finally untie her, Jenny can't stop embracing me. She is extremely tender all night, and the next day too. It's hard to abandon my role: I'm more authoritative with her for quite some time.

The next week I remember Ricky Weldon and inquire about him.

"One of my brightest students," she says.

"Have there been any more advances?"

"A few melting gazes . . ."

"Which you do your best to encourage."

"Certainly not! It's bad for the class dynamics."

I change the subject. "What were the other daydreams about?"

"Mostly fame and money," she says. "It's an all-American class."

We decide to play Fantasy Come True at regular intervals—"At the end of every month," suggests Jenny, "so we'll have something to look forward to all month."

"Okay," I say. Actually, there's only one fantasy which really excites me, but I know Jenny would never agree to it.

SKIN

For December, I decide to repeat her last fantasy—the other way around. She liked bondage so much, it made me curious, so I have her tie me up.

But she bungles the job. I keep having to tell her what to do, yet one belt is so tight, my left hand is turning red, and the other so loose I could get free in seconds. Jenny apologizes and giggles nervously. Then she starts to fondle me. It works, I am hard. She goes to the kitchen and gets a bowl of ice cream. Not touching me, she eats the ice cream, very slowly and sensually. I'm not sure which I want more: some Häagen-Dazs vanilla or some sexual relief. At last she sits down on me, and moves. I get off all right, but it isn't very special, more like an underground explosion far away: weak, muffled. I'm eager for her to get off (both ways!) so I can get my left hand free.

"I'm sorry, honey," she says as she unties me.

"It was fine," I say gallantly. "Interesting."

I am the masseur in January, and Jenny lies naked beneath me as I rub coconut oil into her back. I've been massaging her body for forty-five minutes, and I'm getting tired. I move my hands down and knead the cheeks of her buttocks. I love the substantial spring and roll of a good behind. Too bad the skin is always so rough there from sitting. I apply more oil to the area and think of how great it would be if the female ass had as fine a texture as the female breast. I rub her inner thighs, my fingers as if inadvertently brushing her cunt. After teasing her awhile, I turn her on her back and part her legs with professional exactitude.

"I think you need some internal massage, madame, but that's fifty dollars extra." I'm improvising on the theme, and she loves it.

"Certainly," she says. "Go right ahead."

I gently move my fingers into her body and rhythmically explore. Jenny is breathing hard, and soon it will be too late.

I remove my hand. "You may prefer this, madame," I say, and let her have some dick. I pull out before she can come, and she emits a cry of protest.

I say, "Turn over, please." She gives me a reproachful look before she turns to lie on her stomach. I enter her from behind. Snugly lodged, I rest one hand against her mouth and the other hand on her clit and start a bilateral massage. Within seconds, Jenny explodes—and I do too. Curled like spoons, we fall asleep at once.

Later, Jenny snuggles against me. "Paul, you're just terrific," she whispers. "I'll do anything for you next month."

But would she? I wonder. What are the limits of our game? And can more than two play? For what I really want is a threesome: Jenny and me and some lovely young thing, all doing things to each other at once. Now, *that* would sure be a Fantasy Come True! But Jenny has never shown any sexual interest in women, and I don't want to suggest something she might find repugnant. And I worry about escalating our play into real decadence.

Then again, who started it? Who was the teacher?

Through most of February I'm preoccupied with, and exhausted by, the Lawrence malpractice suit, and Jenny, too, seems tired a lot. So we don't make love much this month, and when we do, there's no spillover from the masseur enactment, as there was from the bondage episode. Sexually, we're just idling, and that's okay with me. It's part of the cycle, I guess.

But one day I notice a small scratch on her shoulder. "What's that?" I ask.

"That?" She looks and shrugs. "Beats me. Isn't it funny how one acquires bruises without knowing how?"

"That's not a bruise, it's a scratch."

"Well, it's a very little one. I probably did it with my hairbrush."

"Your *hairbrush*?" And I start to worry about her students

again, about afternoon studies in the bedroom. When I was seventeen, I could come three times an hour. I picture Jenny and some handsome young stud in lengthy, vigorous conjunction. But no, impossible. Maybe she's just having a flirtation. She certainly looks terrific before she sets off for school. I ask how Ricky Weldon's doing. She shrugs.

"Ricky's not in my class anymore."

"What did you give him last term?"

She blushes. "Ninety-seven."

"*What?*"

"Ricky was my best writer," she says, enunciating primly. "The mark was entirely justified."

Was it? Could she? Now that he wasn't in her class anymore, would she? But she's not turned on by younger guys. She says.

A week later, as I return from work, I run into Mrs. Francis, our upstairs neighbor, in the hall. She is holding our fondue pot, which she borrowed from us last night.

"Oh, good," says Mrs. Francis, seeing me. "I was worried you might need this."

As if we have fondue every night.

"I came down with it at four, but no one answered the bell," she continues. She hands me the pot. "I thought I heard voices, but . . ." Her voice trails off. "Thanks a lot, now."

"You're welcome." Nosy bitch, I add silently.

I put down the pot and unlock the door. Silence. I prowl through the apartment and discover Jenny napping in bed. She awakens as I enter the bedroom and stretches up naked arms to hug me. I kiss her briefly.

"Have you been home all afternoon?" I ask, trying to be casual.

"Uh-huh. I made us a casserole—and then I got tired. Turkey tetrazzini."

One of my favorites. "Great." Pause. "Any visitors?"

"Visitors?" She frowns.

"I ran into Mrs. Francis with that damned fondue pot, and she says she heard voices and rang the bell at four, but nobody came to the door."

"Strange."

"Isn't it?"

"I guess the radio was on too loud. Sometimes when I'm cooking with the radio on, I can't hear that inner bell."

"Was it a talk show?"

"No. Music."

"Then what about the voices she heard?"

"Maybe the announcers. Or some ad. Paul, what is this— the Inquisition?"

"I don't know *what* it is."

She replies, "It's your fevered imagination. Speaking of which, do you realize, it's already February twenty-seventh? Tonight's a good night for it." For Fantasy Come True, she means.

She gets up and pulls on some jeans and a sweater. Then she departs for the kitchen. I sit at the desk, wondering what the hell she was doing this afternoon and why the hell I should deny my desires if she simply gratifies hers. I take out the pad and write what I really want from her tonight. I put the paper in an envelope and place it on the coffee table.

Jenny says, "Is that it?"

"After dinner."

"Aw, pweeze," she says, being cutesy, and I am doubly glad I wrote what I did. I shake my head.

She says, "Just tell me whether I'm going to be your masseuse."

"Nope. I *do* have some ideas of my own, you know. Now, where's this dinner?"

Dinner is terrific. I'm glad she didn't open the envelope

beforehand, for it would have been a shame to have spoiled the meal with angry words. We do the dishes together. I am eager to cooperate with her if she is willing to cooperate with me.

We return to the living room. I light a cigarette. "Now?" she asks.

I nod, and she opens the envelope. She reads:

> A threesome. You, me, and some beautiful woman. You both make love to me. Then you make love to each other. Then me again.

She puts down the paper and says nothing.

I remind her, "You said last month you'd do anything."

"Would you ever do it for me?"

"What?"

"You, me, and a guy."

"Of course not!"

"So?"

I tell her, "I never said I'd do *anything*."

She nods solemnly. "That's true." My wife is a very fair woman. There is silence. Then she says, softly. "Okay."

"What?"

"Okay."

"You mean that?"

"Yeah, sure." She is grinning, or trying to. "Why not?"

"You won't find it too awful?" Now that I have her consent, I am suddenly concerned about her feelings.

"I don't think so," she says.

She'll do it! For me! I am no longer angry at Jenny: I am grateful, and eager for our adventure to begin.

"Look," I tell her. "I have the names of some bars here. This sort of thing is quite common, you know." I have thought it all out: we are an attractive couple, and at one of the swingers clubs downtown we should be able to meet someone who'll come home with us.

Jenny says, "A bar?" She wrinkles her nose. "How tawdry!"

"Well, where else?" I ask. "The personals?"

"I might know someone," she tells me. "Let me make a telephone call."

"Someone who's done this sort of thing before?"

Jenny nods. I'm amazed. I ask, "Is she pretty?"

"She's beautiful."

"Go call her."

She disappears into the bedroom and closes the door for privacy. Where can Jenny know this woman from? Sandra's crowd? Sandra is Jenny's sister, an actress—but surely Jenny won't involve her family in her sex life.

Jenny returns. "She's coming over in half an hour."

"Really? That's terrific! I just can't believe it!"

"Let's have a drink," says Jenny. "I need it."

"Of course. You poor thing. You're being just wonderful, Jenny. You know, if you're nervous, we don't *have* to . . ."

"We don't have to, but we will," she says firmly. "It's only fair." She's probably thinking that so far she has received much more pleasure from Fantasy Come True than I have, and she's right. So far, that is.

We drink some wine, and I tell her that I love her. I stroke her hair. We talk about where we should go over spring vacation. Finally, the downstairs buzzer rings.

I leap up to answer it. Then I open the apartment door and look down the stairwell to see who's coming up.

She is dark-haired, white-skinned, thin, young, exquisite. She has very short hair and many earrings in one ear. She smiles up at me with a mixture of shyness and eagerness that is ineffably poignant.

"Hello," I say, dazzled.

"You must be Paul," she says on the landing. Again, that smile. "I've heard so much about you."

She has? She walks into the apartment, and I close the door behind her. I can't quite believe how lucky I am, how well this is all working out.

But because I'm a lawyer, I have to learn something at once, before things go any further. I sit down at one end of the couch and ask, "How old are you?"

She says, "I just turned eighteen."

That's a relief.

She says, glancing at Jenny, "Jennifer and I were just celebrating . . ."

They *were*? When? How? I ask, "What's your name?"

"Ricky," she says as she sits down beside me. "Ricky Weldon."

The Perfect Aphrodisiac

D R. ALFRED HOFFER—SCIENTIST, moralist, paterfamilias—couldn't understand what was happening. It was an April afternoon, and he was riding home from his laboratory at the Mendoz Research Center in Basel, Switzerland, just as he always did. Yet everything seemed different. The well-known streets seemed to pulse and beckon; the air was luminous and pink; and his bicycle kept wobbling beneath him. Dr. Hoffer felt very strange. His mouth was dry; his hands were burning; and he was pedaling, unsteadily, around an enormous erection.

When he got home, he found his wife at the sink, peeling potatoes. Margaret Hoffer was stout and gray. Dr. Hoffer aproached her eagerly, exultantly. Then he made love to her in the kitchen, on the stairs, in the hall, and, as an afterthought, in the bedroom.

It was many hours before the fifty-two-year-old chemist could ponder upon these events. But at dawn, in the afterglow of ecstasy, his mind was clear. He remembered that the day before he'd been working with a newly discovered family of alkaloids, isolating one isomer, MFB, that had never been tested. Somehow, while preparing it, he must have ingested some of the chemical. Somehow, the substance made eros flower within. Somehow, in one of those accidents for which science is famous, he had chanced upon the perfect aphrodisiac.

HOMO SAPIENS OR HOMO SEXUALIS?

From the very first, man has sought ways to enhance his sexual pleasure. In fact, it is this very striving that distinguishes our species from the other primate groups. When an archeologist finds an erotic drawing on a cave wall or a sexual device in a midden, he can be sure humans have dwelled in the area.

The quest for greater sexual satisfaction is as old as human history. The Sumerians, the Mayans, the Chinese—all ancient peoples sought aphrodisiacs. For thousands of years, humans have eaten and administered honey, ginseng, oysters, onions, and blood for the purpose of augmenting sexual joy.[1] Indeed, aphrodisiacal claims have been made for any substance which resembles the sex organs (carrots, parsnips, mushrooms[2]), which inflames the mucous membranes (mustard, garlic, "Spanish fly"), or which is generally exotic. Among the more esoteric items ingested in hopes of augmenting coition are crocodile kidneys fancied by the Elizabethans and hippomanes (the fleshy excrescence that appears on a foal's head at birth), treasured by the Greeks.[3]

Like voodoo, any of these aphrodisiacs could be very effective—if one believed in it to begin with. There was no substance, however, which actually worked on its own. MFB promised to change all that.

MFB: BLIGHT OR BLESSING?

Still holding his good wife, Dr. Hoffer lay underneath the feather comforter and wondered what to do with his findings. He was not a hedonistic man, and it was not a hedonistic age. His discovery might bring scorn and shame upon him and his family. Who knew how MFB might blight the reputations of his daughters or ruin the careers of his sons. Jean-Louis was an international banker; Henri-Paul was a professor at a Catholic college; Claude-Marc was a bellboy at a three-star hotel.

Dr. Hoffer saw at once that MFB posed a moral problem and a civic threat. He imagined MFB being given to children or nuns; he pictured family gatherings turning into orgies; he foresaw MFB depraving Switzerland, Europe, the world. Perhaps he should simply ignore the drug and proceed with the anti-asthma experiments using another isomer. No one would know.

His wife stirred in his arms. Dear Margaret. He hadn't felt such tenderness toward her in years. He mused on how selfless she was, how deeply good, how excellent a pastry cook. It would be nice to let her try this MFB sometime. How surprised (and *pleased*) she'd been the night before.

And now it seemed to Dr. Hoffer that far from having stumbled upon an agent of evil, he had found a force for the good. MFB would make people everywhere more loving, more humane. His discovery would directly and immediately increase human happiness—and how many scientists could aver as much? Although the room was light now, and the birds were chirping, Dr. Hoffer fell into a contented doze.

Margaret let him sleep until ten, when she brought his favorite breakfast to the bed and kissed him awake. He confided his discovery to her and told her his hopes and his fears.

But publication of his paper[4] earned Dr. Hoffer neither

notoriety nor acclaim. For several years his findings were simply ignored. Europe had pressing economic and social problems to solve. MFB seemed irrelevant, and Dr. Hoffer continued his researches without arousing the attention of his fellow scientists.

PATIENTS AND PRISONERS

Four years after Dr. Hoffer's discovery, however, Douglas Clauson, a young English psychiatrist, began successfully administering minute amounts of MFB to a group of severely withdrawn patients. In fourteen out of fifteen cases, the drug enabled the patients "to establish better links with their spouses and the real world."[5] (In the fifteenth case, the patient fell in love with his hand.)

Two years later, MFB was extensively tested on the men and women of two federal prisons in Mississippi. Overnight guest privileges were extended to those who participated in the program. It became one of the most successful volunteer experiments in the annals of prison medicine. Although the inmates didn't know whether or how MFB might injure them, time after time they selflessly volunteered for the drug. The results showed it to be impressively safe. There seemed to be no harmful side effects from an MFB experience. Indeed, the drug changed body chemistry very little; it merely produced "natural" states of intense arousal and fulfillment. Even administered in excess, MFB did not harm the heart, lungs, liver, or gonads.[6]

MFB was used less successfully on another prisoner—an eighteen-year-old zoo elephant named Lola, who had refused to mate in the several years since achieving her maturity. Perhaps carelessly, perhaps vengefully, the keeper injected Lola with one hundred times the MFB she should have received. Lola gave a mighty blast of pleasure. Then she fell on her knees, as if in gratitude. Fifteen minutes later, she was dead.[7] This tragic episode sparked a general reevaluation of how we treat animals and inspired the first of many books on "speciesism." Nonetheless, the fact remains that there has yet to be a single human MFB o.d.

It is also true that a sensible MFB regimen can sometimes help cure certain types of mental illness. Inspired by Dr. Clauson, a number of mental clinics quietly adopted MFB therapy for use on patients suffering from autism and trauma.

INTO THE LIMELIGHT

Doctors and nurses who observed the drug's effect were eager to try it on themselves and their loved ones, but MFB was hard to obtain. The Mendoz Chemical Corporation was the only company in the world to make the drug, and it required a statement, signed by three doctors, as to the use of each MFB dose ordered. In another unprecedented precautionary measure, Mendoz didn't manufacture MFB in tablet or pill form. Instead, the drug came in a bright green, pungent-tasting liquid, eight ounces to the dose. This was to prevent accidental or "surprise" MFB episodes that unrequited lovers might arrange with stolen "lime," as the drug came to be called. (In certain circles, it was also known as "big green.") Despite all precautions, however, a number of people, mainly researchers and intellectuals, were trying MFB for their own enjoyment.

Manfred Malsey was prominent among these early users. Twenty-five years earlier, Malsey had written a powerful novel about a future society that depended upon "jima" (a synthetic aphrodisiac) for procreation, recreation, and incentive. The young Malsey had obvious contempt for the lotus-eaters he had created; his book, which remains preeminent among anti-Utopian novels, is bitter, even scathing.

As he aged, however, Manfred Malsey mellowed—and, of

course, his sexual powers waned. At fifty-five, he was delighted to learn that his wholly imagined "jima" existed; far from despising MFB, he and his wife immediately set out to obtain some. The first time, they took it under discreet medical supervision; the second time, they just took it; the third time, they took it with Malsey's mistress. Malsey became MFB's leading champion. His intelligent and lyrical account of his lime sessions, *Behind the Green Door*,[8] proved a persuasive introduction to the drug for thousands of artists, musicians, and assorted pleasure-seekers.

GREEN TOWARD GOD

Soon, as with any man-made commodity, the demand created the supply. A few chemistry graduate students at Harvard began making their own MFB—less pure and less potent than Mendoz's, but still strong enough to change the coldest individual to a fervid lover. It was this bootleg MFB—still colored a bright green and a half a pint a hit—that was used in thousands of lime rituals over the next five years.

For rituals they were: during this period, no one treated the drug as a mere thrill. A sexadelic session was as carefully planned as a wedding, as a memoir of the era reveals:

> Emmett and I spent several weeks in preparation. We read and discussed the principal works of William Blake, William James, and William Carlos Williams. We ate only perfectly balanced yin-yang meals. We hung mirrors, arranged pitures, and gathered costumes and toys to place near the bed. We wanted our MFB experience to yield us the deepest emotions, the richest perceptions.[9]

The "limeheads" of the time were serious, ceremonial, and even religious in their use of the drug. At the very least, they expected to "merge" with their partner(s); at the most, they hoped to merge with God.

GEARING UP IN NEW HAVEN

Nonetheless, it wasn't until Wellerby Gearing began his experiments at Yale and enjoined his students to "learn from the loins" that MFB aroused national attention. Gearing might have remained just another academic crank if he hadn't been so handsome. On meeting him, several reporters immediately decided that their stories would be more authentic if they took lime *with* Mr. Gearing, who was never known to refuse. The resultant accounts were not exactly objective, but the MFB experience, aficionados insisted, demanded another mode than the dry detachment then in journalistic favor. A new style of involved and personal reporting began:

> Wellerby Gearing held out the glass. The green liquid shimmered in front of me. I was scared shitless. What if it changed me forever? Or what if I didn't even get off? How would that change my self-image as New Jersey's leading sensualist? I drank, I waited. Gearing left the room. And then in the toes I felt it first. I kicked off my shoes, my feet were naked and awakened, arches aching, almost crying to be filled. I curled my foot around my fist, but it wasn't enough. I wanted more, deeper, harder.[10]

What came to be known as the New Journalism was a direct result of the MFB phenomenon.

Meanwhile, the increasingly flamboyant Gearing was presiding over sexadelic sessions every week—sometimes with his students. It didn't take long for the deans and trustees at Yale to fire this "brazen priest of lust."[11] Wellerby Gearing and his followers (secretly subsidized by a leading publisher and a playboy senator) withdrew to a three-hundred-acre estate in Vermont. There they edited the *Sexadelic Review* and lobbied for free love and MFB. Six months later, Gearing was arrested for cannabis possession and income tax evasion. He was sentenced to ten years in jail. That week, there were protests at Yale, Berkeley, Columbia, and Herkimer Community College.

LIMEOUTS REAL AND RUMORED

Every movement needs a martyr, and with Gearing in prison, lime was the latest cause. All over America, tart green punch was served at trendy parties to "simulate what stimulates." Sometimes, however, real lime was secretly substituted for the false. This subterfuge was known as "sub-liming" one's guests. It was amusing to note who managed to observe the social niceties while high on lust—and who did not. It was a kind of test—a test a few unfortunates failed. Jack R. Buck, for instance, jumped out of a window, leaving a note saying that he was going "insane from syphilis or masturbation."[12] (Luckily, it was only a first-story window.) Other distraught individuals (mainly *naïfs* who had wandered into large and sophisticated parties) had to be taken to hospital emergency rooms, where they were confined to straitjackets for twelve hours, or until the drug wore off.

Meanwhile, MFB was implicated in the starvation death of an amorous couple; in the blinding of a woman who made love on a beach while staring at the sun; and in widespread chromosomal changes among college students.[13] The first two stories have been thoroughly discredited; and it has since been conclusively shown that the average cup of coffee inflicts more genetic damage than a dose of MFB.

Many observers believed that the government had fostered the antilime rumors, for people who took the drug bought less, smiled more, and were generally uncooperative about civic responsibilities. They tended to be tax evaders and draft dodgers. Freud had written in *Civilization and Its Discontents* that the repression of the individual libido is essential to community formation; now the FBI reported that lime was undermining the American Way of Life.

Lime enthusiasts, however, claimed that MFB was man's best hope for the future. Their largest demonstration, at the Pentagon, drew half a million young people chanting "Make love, not war" and performing such flagrant love acts that it was impossible to broadcast footage of their protest.

MFB AND MARRIAGE

More persuasive than any demonstration, however, was Barry Brent's testimony on late night TV. Brent, who for two generations had personified suavity and charm for moviegoers around the world, now confessed that before his MFB therapy he had been a "self-centered boor."[14] His drug sessions, he explained, had enabled him to be "genuinely sensitive to the needs of others" and to "open up in new ways." "MFB has changed my marriage and my life," he announced, eyes glowing, smile gleaming.

Naturally, his revelations only increased the demand for the drug, especially among the maritally challenged. One expert claims that in the next three years, MFB helped save half a million ailing marriages.[15] Another expert counters that in the same period, MFB caused 200,000 divorces.[16]

GREEN PROFITS AND LIME CRIMES

Either way, MFB was becoming big business. Recognizing the demand for the drug, and dropping all pretense about duplicating the Mendoz product, organized crime began manufacturing and distributing MFB—in tablets. "Big green" became instantly obsolete, and the MFB crime wave began. Call girls slipped the drug to their clients—then charged them extra for each sexual act. Students sneaked it into the teachers' coffee machine and gathered to watch the results. Radicals were apprehended trying to place it in the Senate cafeteria water supply.

Dr. Hoffer's worst premonitions were coming true. For months, acute paranoia reigned across America. The fourteen-year-old girl drinking a Coke on her first date; the newspaper editor sipping water during a televised conference; the grandparents of visiting long-haired teens: all were equally worried about possible MFB poisoning. In a special address to the nation, the President announced that he was "launching a crash program"[17] to find an MFB antidote and win the war on lime.

Within months, the FDA approved an MFB antidote. "Nonsex" worked by inducing an intense nausea in the individual. This drug was rarely used, for most people felt that it was better to make love with the most bizarre characters, in the most inappropriate settings, than to vomit alone by the hour. The second FDA-approved MFB antidote, borzine, proved more acceptable: it combatted MFB quickly and effectively with no side effects other than producing chilly fingers and toes (the "cold feet" syndrome). With a few tabs of borzine stocked in the medicine cabinet (or handy in the pocket), Americans began to feel secure again.

The Fading of the Green

By this time, however, lime fever was cooling on its own. Several million Americans had already tried the drug, and intellectuals were sneering that the MFB ecstasy was "too easy."[18] The media were bored with the drug. College students were discovering that although one MFB trip could be a revelation, the second one was just a repetition, and the third could be downright boring. All those intense psychogenital sensations *again* . . . It was considered hip to have *taken* MFB—but not to "need" it anymore. Now if one's lover offered lime, the correct stance was outrage, as in the following scene from a novel of the time.

> She threw the tablets to the floor.
> "What's wrong?' he asked.
> "Don't you think I'm good enough without that phony crap?"
> "But, Claudia . . ."
> "Get out. You make me sick!"[19]

Disco dancing, platform shoes, and a high grade-point average displaced MFB among the interests of the young. Wellerby Gearing, released at last, was derided and pitied, an outmoded figure from another epoch.

Lime was thoroughly discredited when *The New York Times* revealed that fifteen years earlier, the CIA had been using MFB as a "disorienting" agent. After that, only a few diehards, who maintained that anything that felt so good had to be right, continued to take lime, but they had considerable trouble getting supplies. Organized crime now concentrated on other drugs, and it became easier to find heroin or cocaine than to get MFB. The "greening" of America was over.

FATHER LIME TODAY

And what of Dr. Alfred Hoffer? Was he persecuted and reviled? Did "Father Lime" die brokenhearted and alone? Not at all. The Swiss are a tolerant people, and they recognized the accidental nature of his discovery. Although Mendoz ceased production of MFB several years ago, the company has always treated Dr. Hoffer with respect, refusing to blame him for the consequences of his findings. His pension is handsome; he and his wife, both in their nineties, continue to live a comfortable life in Basel. They are an extraordinarily lively and affectionate old couple; they look decades younger than they are.

One recent afternoon, a visiting academic inquired as to their secret. Albert Hoffer smiled. Margaret Hoffer blushed.

---

[1] Ezekiel Wedeck, *Love Potions Through the Ages: A Study of Amatory Devices and Mores*. New York: Philosophical Library.

[2] Charles Connel, *Aphrodisiacs in Your Garden*. London: A. Barker.

[3] Wedeck, *op.cit.*

[4] Alfred Hoffer, "MFB: *Eine Vorbesprechung*," *Helvetica Chimica Acta*, Vol. 26, No. 3. Basel.

[5] Douglas Clauson, "A New Approach to Melancholia," *British Journal of Psychiatry*, Vol. 95, No. 9. London.

[6] Thomas Lovett, "MFB: Aphrodisiac for Today," *American Journal of Sexual Behavior*, Vol. 3, No. 2. San Francisco.

[7] "The Elephant and the Ecstasy," *Time*, Vol. 35, No. 17.

[8] Manfred Malsey, *Behind the Green Door: The Joy of Jima*. London: Chatto and Windus.

[9] Annie Stein Knobler, *The Year of the Goat*. New York: Knopf.

[10] Gonzo Rubenstein, "Day-tripping with Wellerby Gearing," *The Village Voice*, Vol. 7, No. 12.

[11] Arthur Woodridge IV, "An Unfortunate Episode," *The Yale Alumni Magazine*, Vol. 25, No. 8. New Haven, Conn.

[12] Ben Ruff, "Green Alert: Lime Strikes in Syosset," *Daily News* New York, Vol. 50, No. 147.

[13] Martha Cashin-Fast, *The MFB Story*. New York: Morrow.

[14] "The New Barry Brent: World Enough and Lime," *Life*, Vol. 26, No. 4.

[15] I. C. Rozie, *Sexual Ties and the Marriage Knot*. New York: Crown.

[16] Nan Van Shannon, " 'Green' Therapy: A Jaundiced Look," *Journal of Family and Marriage Counseling*, Vol. 4, No. 1.

[17] Jerry G. Lee, *Presidential Bloopers*. New York: Press Press.

[18] Susan Hardwich, "Lime in Our Time: or the Facile and the Docile," *Atlantic Monthly*, Vol. 113, No. 8.

[19] J. D. Lynn, *The Quadrangle*. New York: Macmillan.

Fingers

THE PHONE RINGS WHILE I'M MOPPING the floor.

He says, "I had the sexiest dream about you last night."

"Really?" The voice is familiar, but I can't quite place it. I lean the mop against the wall.

He says, "Just the sexiest dream."

I start pouring this morning's coffee from the decanter into a mug. I ask, "Who is this?"

"Aw, come on, you know who this is."

"No, really, I'm sorry, I'm not good at voices. You'll just have to tell me." I'm suddenly worried.

"I don't believe this! I really don't."

His indignation reassures me: this is no demented stranger. I put the coffee in the microwave.

"All right," he says. "I'll give you a hint. I've been out of town for a while."

So it's okay that I don't know his voice—but who is it?

And then, and I'm just grinning into the phone, I know it's my college boyfriend, Lenny, who's moved to California. "Lenny!" I sing. "Hey, how *are* you?"

"All *right*! Look, I just have to tell you about this incredible dream!"

"Lenny, it's so great to hear from you! Are you here for long? Am I going to see you? We can all get together if you want, or just you and me . . ." Which is what I want most, but we're both married now, grown-ups.

"Don't you want to know about my dream?"

"You know, you frightened me before. How did I know it wasn't some pervert, some maniac calling from the phone booth on my corner?"

He says, "Don't be so paranoid."

But I realize—and my hand slips as I take the coffee out of the microwave—that I don't know it's Lenny at all. I called him that; he merely agreed. I pull aside the kitchen curtain and look out. There's no one in the phone booth on the corner. I sponge off the coffee which I spilled on the counter.

"Don't you want to know about my dream?" Wherever he is, he sounds warm, relaxed, and he is laughing softly.

"I'm not sure. I'm really not sure." Lenny did laugh like that though—when he was stoned. I no longer smoke dope, but it used to be fun to do it with him. "Lenny, are you high? You sound high."

"Of course not, I'm at work. Now, listen. You're sitting in this chair, and you're wearing a very short, tight dress. And you know how it is, how when you sit down your skirt rises. So you're just sitting there, with your dress very high on your legs . . ."

"Lenny, stop, I'm getting all nervous again. Before you go any further, you just have to tell me something so I know it's really you. Some proof for my paranoia."

I want him to say "Grand Central Baths." The last time

I saw Lenny, I was three months pregnant with Mozelle. Lenny and I were in a cafe in Berkeley, and he turned to me and said, "Sarah, how would you like a warm bath?"

On the phone now he says, and I can tell he's hurt, "I just don't believe this. Really, Susan."

"*Susan?* This isn't Susan."

"Not Susan!"

"No. I'm sorry." He makes me feel, for the moment, to blame. Then I remember, and hear myself wailing, "But you said you were Lenny! Why did you say that?"

"Because my name *is* Lenny! Lenny Paulson."

"Damn. Not Lenny Baxter." And no one is dreaming about me sitting in a chair, in a very short skirt.

"You sound just like Susan," he says reproachfully.

"You sound a lot like Lenny. *My* Lenny, I mean."

"Do you want to hear my dream anyway?"

"Why would I want to hear the dream of some stranger?"

"Come on. What were you doing when I called?"

"Mopping the floor."

"Well, this has to be better than that!"

"Oh, all right. Tell me your dream. But I have to warn you, I'm the nervous type, I may just hang up. . . ."

"You don't sound like the nervous type."

"How do I sound?"

"You sound terrific."

I am silent. Tears of gratitude come to my eyes. It feels like I've been a wife and mom forever.

"Come on," Lenny says. "Imagine the odds against all this! The Lenny confusion. You sounding like Susan. It's fate! You have to hear out this dream."

I remain silent.

He persists. "What—do I sound dangerous?"

"No, actually, you sound very nice." I think of Jennifer, my best friend. She wants to meet a nice man, settle down, have a couple of kids. But there's such a shortage of good men! I should find out more about this Lenny Paulson. "I was just wondering, if you were married or . . ."

"I'm divorced," he said. "What about you?"

"I'm married."

"You are?" he says, surprised.

"Uh-huh. How old are you? You sound about my age— I'm thirty-five." The words sound bald; anonymity has made me blunt.

"I'm thirty-eight," he says. "An attorney."

"I work at home," I say. "I'm an editor."

"When you're not mopping the floor."

"Or doing the laundry."

"How tall are you?" he asks. "In the dream, you're five feet eight."

"I'm five five. Anyway, you had this dream about Susan, not me. Tell it to Susan!"

"Now, now, don't be jealous. Just let me tell it to you first."

"Okay."

"So you're sitting there in this chair, see, with your dress very high—and what happens next?"

"God, I don't know—it's your dream, and I've never even met you!"

"Well, I'm staring at your legs, getting a really good look at your panties—and what do *you* do?"

I'm suddenly frightened again.

He asks, "What's your name?"

This does not allay my fears. "No," I say, "I'm not telling."

"No fair—you know mine."

"Guess I'm chicken."

"All right. So you're in this chair," he says, and pauses.

I am in that chair, I have always been in that chair. . . .

He laughs softly. "And I'm looking up your legs . . . and, go on, tell me what you do."

I think of what Jennifer might do if she was just a little drunk and she liked the guy. "Well, I just might say, 'Enjoying the view?'"

"Oh, God—yes, Mrs. Wilkerson, I'll put the documents in the mail today." And—click—he hangs up the phone. Clearly, someone walked in on him.

What happened next in the dream? Was the chair part of the proceedings? Did the short, tight dress come off, or was it just pushed aside? Did he kneel between my legs, that is, *Susan's* legs, and apply his mouth? Or was this all about eyes and fingers?

Now that he's hung up, I'm convinced he'd be a hit with Jennifer. He has that lovely, soft laugh.

That time, in Berkeley, I told Lenny, *my* Lenny, "Look, I'm embarrassed, my waist is thick, my breasts are big."

"You look great," he said. "You'll love it, Sarah."

At Grand Central Baths, you rent your own room and lock it. You get your own hot tub and shower and bench for lying on and drying out or making love. He said early pregnancy suited me. He said my breasts were sensational. He said he often thought of our nights in my dorm.

When we came out of the bath, he dried me off tenderly, touched me here and there, and eased himself into me. When he was well and wholly lodged, he smiled down and said, "Remembrance of things past." Then he began to move.

It was instantly apparent that his education had continued without me. He had always been eager; now he had finesse. He'd learned this way of corkscrewing slowly on the downstroke . . . I'm not usually multiorgasmic, but I was with Lenny Baxter that afternoon at the baths.

Because he was an old boyfriend, it wasn't really adultery. He said as we left, "For the next six months, you can have this to think about," and he was right, I kept those hours secret and brought them out to comfort me when I felt bulky and ignored.

Now Mozelle is three. When I return to the mopping, the water in the pail's gone cold. After I finish the floor, I try information. There's no listing for a Lenny Paulson. He could live anywhere, of course, but I get the feeling he's right here in the city and hasn't settled in yet.

A week later, I call information again. This time I get a new listing for a Leonard Paulson uptown. I carry the number in my wallet for three days. When I pay for anything, I feel the hidden paper warm my hands.

I keep all this a secret from Jennifer, not wanting to raise her hopes prematurely.

After dinner my husband asks if I want to see the movie that's playing around the corner. "Not really," I say. "But you go ahead." We sometimes go singly to successive shows when we can't get a sitter.

"You're sure you don't mind?"

"No, I'm fine, I've got a good book."

At ten o'clock I make the call. He picks up on the second ring. "Hello?"

"I had . . . the sexiest dream about you last night."

"Who is this?"

"Well, I'm not Susan. And last time we spoke, you were enjoying the view."

"Well, *hello*. But you never told me your name."

"It's Sarah. Are you alone?"

"Yes, why?"

"I have to tell you my dream."

"I'm thrilled," he says. "You looked me up. You're pursuing me."

"It's not like you imagine," I say, thinking about Jennifer.

"How do you mean? Why did you call?"

"I just had to hear how your dream ended. The one about Susan sitting in a chair. Who's Susan anyway?"

"She's an old girlfriend."

"Have you seen her yet? Since we spoke?"

"Why, yes."

"What was that like?"

"Weird. She's gained forty pounds and her hair's gone gray. I just can't get over it. . . ."

"People change fast at our age. Unless they're careful."

"I'm careful," he says.

"I'm careful too." The word seems multileveled. "Now don't you want to hear *my* dream?"

"I'm the nervous type," he says. "I just may hang up on you."

But he is laughing softly, the way Lenny did at Grand Central Baths when I lowered my head into the water. He says, "Look, is this dream about me or the other Lenny?"

"I don't know for sure. What do you look like?" He's as jealous of the other Lenny as I was of Susan!

"How was I in your dream?"

"Fantastic."

"In appearance, I mean."

"Five ten, curly-haired, thin."

"I'm six two," he says, "but otherwise, that's right. I've got blue eyes and a big nose and, Sarah, I've got this big, thick—"

I hang up, bang. My heart is beating fast. I make myself some mint tea. It's comforting to know that he can't call me back—but I can always get to him. I have a feeling Jennifer would like this tall man who talks dirty.

Ten minutes later he calls me back. "Hello, Sarah."

"How did you get my number?

"I've been calling variations on Susan's number. One number up and down each digit. This is my thirteenth call."

"My, how resourceful."

"I'm sorry about before. It must be scary, dirty talk from a stranger. I won't do it again, I promise. Now I want to know about this dream."

I hear a key in the lock. "I have to hang up, my husband's home."

"I'll call you tomorrow morning at eleven. Remember, Sarah—now I have your number too."

The next morning, while Max and Mozelle are in school, I wash my hair and give myself a manicure, applying three coats of polish to each nail. The polish is dry when the telephone rings. "Hello?"

"You know who this is."

"Yes, Lenny." It's eleven-eleven, a magic number, four ones lined up in a row. . . .

"Tell me about your dream."

I give him one of Jennifer's fantasies. "We're somewhere on a beach. You're lying on your back, in the sun, wearing a small red bathing suit."

"Red? Why is it red?

"I don't know, it just is. Anyway, I'm sitting near you, looking down at you. Do you know what you do?"

"No, what do I do?"

"Guess."

"Well, I bring you down on top of me, don't I?"

"Yes. Your skin is so warm, Lenny."

"Sarah. God. When can we meet?"

"We can't. I told you. I'm married."

"You just want a telephone turn-on?"

"It's not that. I thought of you for my best friend."

"What?" His voice rises indignantly. "This is all about fixing me up with some blind date?"

"Jennifer is not 'some blind date'! She's beautiful, sensitive, intelligent, warm. And she happens to be five foot eight."

"And you want her to meet with some stranger? For all you know some lunatic?"

"Come on. You're not crazy."

"How can you tell from the phone?"

"I just can. But you're right. Perhaps it's not fair to just throw you together. Perhaps you'd be all wrong for her. I should find out more about you."

"That's why we should meet," he says. "How about tonight?"

"Tonight? I can't just come to your *apartment*. . . ."

"Then come to my office tomorrow," he says. "I have some time at one-thirty. And I'll tell you the end of my dream."

The next day it's raining, so I hail a cab, although I'm short of cash this week. The things I do for Jennifer! I take out my compact and apply more lipstick as I ride uptown.

A secretary brings me into his office, which is very large and like a living room. I see him sitting behind the desk. He looks up with a smile.

It isn't Lenny Baxter, it's this whole new person Lenny Paulson—yet I feel like I've known him forever. I start smiling too, he's so appealing. He's wearing a blue tie the exact color of his eyes. Behind me, I hear the secretary leave and close the door.

Lenny stands up and comes toward me. "Hello, Sarah," he says. "Wow! Thank you, Ma Bell. Thank you, errant fingers."

I say, "Listen, Lenny. You understand. I'm only here to interview you for my friend. And I can't stay very long."

"You can at least take off your coat."

I shake my head. "I'm fine." I'm wearing a long sweater coat.

He's still smiling. "Would you like a drink? Some soda?"

"No, thanks."

"You don't mind if I . . . ?"

"Of course not."

He pours scotch over ice and brings the glass to the coffee

table by the couch. "Sit down," he says, lowering himself onto the couch, but I stay where I am, by the bookcase. "What is it you want to know?"

Your strengths, your hopes, your deepest desires . . . I ask, "Do you have any hobbies?"

"Chess. Squash. Carpentry. Hey, Sarah, why don't you sit down?"

"I'm okay. Really." I'm cruising his books, but they're mainly legal sets, of course.

"Do they pass the test?" he asks confidently.

"Excuse my naked interest," I reply. "You know the saying, 'You are what you read.' "

"I've never heard it that way, but I'd certainly excuse your naked interest. Anytime."

Blushing, I look down at my painted fingernails. I say, "Remember—I'm just the go-between."

"Right. Proceed."

My mind is a blank. I stammer out, "Let's see. Do you have any pets?"

"No—I have children." He hands me a framed portrait of three dark-haired, blue-eyed children who look just like him.

"Didn't your wife have any genetic input?"

"Ex-wife," says Len with a smile in his voice. "Apparently not."

Now that I have the opening, I have to ask the question. "Do you want any more?"

"More kids? No way!"

"But Jennifer wants children!"

"Then it won't work with her," he says, putting down his drink.

"Oh, what a shame."

"Then why are you smiling?"

"I am not!" I feel myself blushing again.

"I bought something today," he says. "When I went out

for lunch." He stands up. "Let me get it." As he passes in back of me, he puts his hand, briefly, on my hair.

My whole head tingles as he rummages inside his desk drawer. I'm suddenly so warm I must take off my sweater coat.

He does something with the door lock and starts walking across the room with a small red garment in his hand. Then he sees me. He stops moving and murmurs, "Oh, baby."

This was never about Jennifer after all.

I'm sitting in a chair with my short, tight dress very high upon my legs. My fingers rest upon my thigh.

I'm about to learn the end of his dream.

Skin

IT SOMETIMES HAPPENS THAT I MEET A woman who has a mole where I do, just above the corner of the mouth. I always notice hers at once, and I can tell that she notices mine; her eyes keep straying to the left side of my face. Mole-sister! I want to say. Do you hide it for the camera? Do you tweeze despite the cancer warnings? Do you worry about it stopping men from kissing you?

We have all been sworn to secrecy about my mother's face-lift: her husband, Jed, her three best friends, and myself. Everyone else thinks she's recovering from a sinus operation, but she's home, in her room, with bruise marks near her eyes and stitches on her face. She sounds extremely cheerful on the phone.

Fifteen years ago, when I was fifteen, I asked a friend's father, a dermatologist, if a mole like mine could be easily removed. He tilted my face to catch the light and said no. This kind of mole, an intradermal nevus, when sliced off could leave a strange pigmented indentation. He said, "Better a mole than a hole."

My mother spent too much time in the sun. Eyes closed, mouth open, she would sprawl, right on the sand, like a starfish on its back. By mid-June she was deeply tanned; in December she still had a bathing suit line. Tomorrow the stitches come out. I shall meet her at her doctor's office to guide her into a cab and back to my apartment. I haven't seen my mother since the operation. She wants to see Tobias.

There it sits, a finger's breadth above my mouth, like a tiny mushroom cap upon my skin. Its color is translucent brown; its texture, waxy, smooth. It feels huge beneath my index finger; the way a canker sore does to the tongue. But against the back of my hand I can scarcely feel it at all. And it may be that not everyone who sees me at close range is especially aware of my mark. Perhaps to some I am not a woman with a mole above her upper lip.

At the fancy grocery store where I buy bread, many women do their marketing in furs. I disapprove of this display of death and wealth, but I love the touch of fur, and when the store is crowded, I hold my hand out so that I can get a feel of the forbidden skins.

I've just measured my mole, in the hope of finding it to be laughably small in dimension, truly insignificant. It is not. It is three-sixteenths of an inch in diameter. If you have a ruler handy, make a line that long right here in the margin. Bisect it with a perpendicular line of equal length, then use the tips of this cross as your guide for making a circle. Now shade it in. You see, now, how my mole asserts itself upon my face. I am not some vain beauty lamenting some imperceptible flaw. On the other hand, my mole is not quite large enough, nor ugly enough, to be truly disfiguring, which just adds guilt to the ruminations it inspires. Maybe I'm making a mountain out of a mole.

Last night I dreamed that my mother had a new fur coat, the most gorgeous coat I had ever seen. The skins were glossy, rich, and smooth; the coat was exquisitely designed. My mother was modeling it for me, walking this way and that, laughing. I reached for the price tag, which was still attached to the sleeve, but she put her hand over it. "Never mind the cost," she said. "How does it look?" "It's okay," I said.

What underlies the need some have to advertise their flaws? Is the motive essentially seductive? Is love me anyway the message, the hope?

My good friend Tess says I should stop worrying about my mole and start celebrating it. She tells me about eighteenth-century English ladies who had a whole wardrobe of beauty marks that they'd glue to their faces provocatively. She points out that a leading fashion model has a mole much like mine. Men find moles sexy, says Tess. I say that perhaps on a great beauty a mole—or any small defect—is humanizing, making the woman approachable, accessible. But I am not a great beauty. You've got beautiful eyes and fabulous legs, says Tess. Ah, but I want great skin—"skin so clear a pencil dot would mar it," as a friend once described his first love. This friend has had problems with his skin all his life. People always want the feature they don't have. Women with straight hair perm it; women with curls try to make their hair lie limp.

SKIN

Months ago I tried to talk my mother out of the face-lift. "You look wonderful, Mom, you always do." But she showed me the lines on her face, then pulled her cheek taut. "How marvelous," she said, "that's what would go." I pointed out the dangers involved; I worried about the anesthesia; I spoke of iatrogenic diseases. "Wouldn't it be stupid if something bad happened because of this vanity surgery?" "I've got a fine doctor," she said, "you needn't worry so." "Well, I don't think you need it. I know you don't." "Wait till you're my age," she said. My mother is fifty-five.

If moles are erotic—which I find highly dubious—perhaps it's because of the color. Some moles, such as mine, are a pinkish-brown shade: the color of lips, nipples, genitalia. My mole sits above my mouth and alludes to my vagina.

In Hawthorne's "The Birthmark," Aylmer, a brilliant man of science, becomes obsessed with the mark of a tiny red hand upon the left cheek of his beautiful wife. When she pales, the mark becomes more distinct: it blazes at him, "a crimson stain upon the snow." Aylmer selects it as "the symbol of his wife's liability to sin, sorrow, decay, and death." Georgina, too, now finds the mark "odious" and begs him to remove it, although "many a desperate swain would have risked life for the privilege of pressing his lips to the mysterious hand." Aylmer devotes himself entirely to removing her birthmark, but all his efforts fail, the mark is so deep. Only one remedy remains, and although it is dangerous, neither hesitates. Aylmer proffers the clear draught to Georgina, and she swallows it at once. And now the birthmark starts to fade from her cheek, and Aylmer rejoices at his power. The mark becomes paler and paler, until it disappears entirely—whereupon, of course, Georgina dies.

I've never asked my husband whether or not my mole disturbs him, but when we sit side by side, I take care to be on his left.

My mother called me a few hours after the surgery. "You can stop worrying," she said. "I'm just fine. Woozy, yes, but fine. And so happy. I'm just so glad I had it done! And do you know what? Right in the middle of the operation, I thought of your little Tobias." "Did you really, Mom? But I don't understand. Didn't they give you general anesthetic?" "No, they just gave me a local." "Well, you should have told me you weren't going under. I was worried about your not coming out." "Stop snapping at me," she replied. "I thought you'd be happy I thought of Tobias." "Yes, of course I am." "And I want to see him as soon as my face isn't frightening. He's the most marvelous baby."

Flaubert, in an essay on esthetics, wondered how a baby would develop if its mother had an ugly birthmark on her breast. Would nursing near a wen or splotch enable that child to see beauty everywhere—or nowhere?

When I arrive at the doctor's office, I'm surprised to find Jed in the waiting room. I knew he was driving her in from New Jersey so she could get the stitches removed, but I thought that afterward he'd be going to work and I'd be with my mother alone. "Hello, Jed." We kiss, and I take off my down jacket. I ask, "How's my mother?" "Excited—and exhausting." We laugh together. Then I walk to the coat rack across the room and hang up my jacket. When I return to him, Jed says, "Now she wants *me* to have a consultation with the doctor." "You? Whatever for?" Jed is short and muscular, with attractive, rugged features. He's been married to my mother for five years. He shrugs. "She says there are bags under my eyes. And folds under my chin. I don't know. She's the one who has to look at me. "Jed, that's ridiculous." My mother comes smiling into the room. Her cheeks look very round and smooth. "Don't kiss me, don't kiss me," she says. "It's still tender." She's wearing sunglasses and she still has some bruises. "Well?" she demands. "Isn't it fabulous?" I say, "You don't look all that different." "That's the point! I think it's just glorious." "Maybe, Mom, but it's hard to tell right now. Your cheeks look a bit mumpy." She says, "They're still swollen. Go on, Jed, he's *waiting*." Jed stands up, winks at me, and disappears down the corridor. I say, "Mom, I think it's very wrong of you to make Jed see your doctor." "I'm not making Jed anything— we both think it's a good idea. He's getting tired of his job, and he's decided to look for something else." "And you think he'll have a better chance after plastic surgery?" "Yes, Muriel—of course he will. Now, tell me—how's your dear Tobias?"

Tobias is two. When he wakes up, he crawls into our bed. He lies upon Steve's chest and croons, "Daddy, daddy, dad." After a while he rolls to me and puts his cheek on mine. "Mommy, mama, mamaze." He straddles my rib cage and looks down on me. "What dat?" he asks, pulling my nose. "You know what that is," I tell him. He is happy to show off his knowledge: "You nose! And what dat? You eye! An here you odder eye!" This is his ritual, and it never varies. "What dese?" he says, pulling at my eyebrow hairs. "You brows! What dis? You mouf!" He forces his fingers between my lips. "And dese you teef," he says. I pretend to bite his hand, and he giggles and pulls it away. But he is not distracted. He grins down at me: he has saved the best for last. "And what dis?" he says, and places his tiny index finger squarely on the mole. No finger but mine has ever touched it directly before, and his moist little fingertip there seems strangely intimate. "What dis, Mom?" Tobias insists. "My beauty mark," I tell him. "Beauty mott, beauty mott! Where mine?" "You don't have one on your face—you have one on your back." He twists around so he can see the raised freckle just above his buttocks. He is only partly consoled. "Little one," he says, "I want bid one. I want one on my face! I want one like dat!" And once more he puts his firm little finger on my mole. It seems his touch goes to my core.

A woman in sunglasses and fur enters the doctor's waiting room from the lobby. She takes a seat near my mother, who gives her a close look and says, "If you're here to have stitches out, don't worry about a thing. It's practically painless. Snip, snip, and they're gone." "Yes, I know," says the woman. "I've done this before." It's impossible to tell how old she is. "Please come this way," the receptionist says, and the woman is gone. My mother turns to me and says, "Now that I've had it done, I can't think why I waited so long. Surely anyone with any joie de vivre wants to keep on looking young." "Nonsense, Mom. Many joyful people don't have face-lifts." She says indignantly, "I didn't *have* a face-lift, I had a mini." "Sorry, sorry." "And the great beauties of the past would have jumped at the chance!" "Cleopatra? Helen of Troy? Pocahontas?" "Why not?" She laughs. Then she frowns. "You know," she says, "you're so pretty. But I wonder if you've ever thought about getting rid of that mole?"

When I think about my mole, it tingles. Is that a sign? A warning? *Cut me out or burn me off, I'll still be with you, Muriel.*

I tell my mother about my friend's father, the dermatologist. "That was fifteen years ago," she says. "Today they can do anything. Why don't you see what my doctor says? My treat. Go on up and make an appointment." My mother gestures with her chin toward the receptionist. I shake my head and say, "Not now." "Surely you don't *like* that thing," she says. Jed comes down the hall. "Well?" my mother asks him. He says, "Well, it's a possibility." She says, "Oh, good, darling, I'm so happy." I cross the room to get my jacket. She says, "And I'm trying to get Muriel to do something about that awful mole." My back is to them as I push my arms into my sleeves. Jed asks, "What awful mole?"

Boss Lady

CONTRARY TO THE LOUCHE REPU-
tation she cultivated, Perri
Wagner, fledgling filmmaker,
former model, total pothead, did not go after every man she
wanted. She had her standards. She would not date the boyfriends or recent ex-boyfriends of her friends, nor the friends
of her present boyfriends. She tried not to sleep with married men and never slept with fathers-to-be.

Perri had no taboos about colleagues or live-ins, however,
so although she had hired Larry Mercator to edit a documentary she was producing, and although rumor had it that
he was living with a high school teacher named Maude, Perri
began eyeing him—especially when she noticed his earring.

Larry wasn't really the earring type. He wore white shirts
and chinos. Yet he had pierced his skin, mutilated his flesh,
so he could wear a gold ring in his ear and be looked at.
Perri began looking at him.

Soon she was beaming at him. That was her word for it,

"beaming." Perri sometimes felt she sent out this current, and she could no more control it, fake it or stop it than decide whether or not it would rain. Since he was by turns hostile and indifferent to her, Perri wished she could stop beaming at Larry. Half wished she could stop. For part of beaming was enjoyment in beaming. It was like getting high. The first symptom was the desire to get higher right away.

Night after night, Peri smoked her midnight joint in bed and thought about Larry. Day after day, she came to the office and beamed and Larry ignored her. Perri was in ecstatic torments about the situation for weeks. The worst thing about an office crush was also the best thing: if it didn't work out, you still had to—or got to—see the person every day. Got to hope, got to agonize. She knew that for her, the agony was essential.

One day, while Perri was in the editing room with Larry, watching him view and mark and cut, a piece of doggerel began forming in her mind. She tried to work out the last of it so she could rip it off her mental notepad and throw it away. Here she was, writing valentines she would never send, elated and alive! She finished the first quatrain:

> His eyes were the color of mag track
> His shirt was the green of Kilgarry
> She sat in the gloom of the editing room
> And tried to write poems to Larry.

When the telephone rang, Perri jumped, but Larry didn't notice. Perri picked up the phone. It was her friend Ann, who knew all about Perri's feelings for Larry. Ann asked, "How's your great crush?"

Perri said, "A little worse than usual today." *He's wearing a new earring.*

Ann asked, "Is he around now?"

"Uh-huh." *I want to creep up on him from behind and put one hand on his mouth and the other on his heart.*

"I hope you're being cool."

I only devour him visually and analyze his every word. Perri said, "Arctic, of course."

"Somehow, I doubt that."

Perri said daringly, looking at the back of Larry's head, "You think he knows?"

Ann said, "Absolutely. You're a terrible actress. You probably blush and stammer a lot when he's around."

Perri took the phone away from her ear and called, "Larry? Do I blush and stammer a lot?"

"Hadn't noticed," Larry said.

"See?" Perri said to Ann.

"I can't believe you. You've gone mad."

"That's nothing." Perri whispered into the phone. "I'll tell you tonight what else I'm going to do."

Ten days later, Perri was aloft, flying to Salt Lake City, toking up in a tiny steel lavatory. She preferred being stoned at takeoff, but there had been no one to drive her to the airport, and there was too much security to smoke in the airport itself. Bathrooms in airplanes always had a No Smoking sign—and a prominent ashtray. The acknowledgment that some would disobey the sign (an ashtray so the bad ones wouldn't start a fire in the trash receptacle) always encouraged Perri to disobey the sign too, even though to do so, she had to disconnect the smoke detector (which was a federal offense, the flight attendant had announced). Perri figured that under the circumstances a joint was no worse than a cigarette. She wondered if constipated nicotine addicts needed a cigarette while moving their bowels. That was the trouble with getting stoned in bathrooms. Your ravings led you shitward. Perri was grateful for the vigorous ventilation system and the equally aggresive air freshener, which mimicked lavender. She combed her hair and decided she needed more color. She put on blusher and lipstick. The bathroom smelled fine when she left, and the walk back to her seat had that special glow, that aura of significance she loved so dearly. . . .

In Salt Lake City, Perri rented a car and drove north for an hour to Park City, a ski town in the mountains. Perri arrived too late for the last movie of the evening, so she picked up her key and went right to her room. Visitors to the Sundance Film Festival were being housed in various places around town, and she was in a spacious condo right at the ski center. In her room, up three broad steps, a hot tub was steaming. She didn't know where Larry was staying and hadn't been able to find out. But she would see him the next evening, at the screening of his film (which he had finished the year before)—if she didn't lose her nerve.

For it suddenly seemed crazy, what she had done. Larry had avoided her for weeks in New York, so she had secretly followed him to Utah in hopes of getting him at last. She sat in the hot tub while the water bubbled around her. If nothing else, she told herself, you're a woman of action. You take command. You want this man and you came to get him—or to know you never will. Boss lady. Yeah!

She reached for the festival program and flipped through the pages. A woman she knew, a director in her forties, was here with her first feature, *Family and Friends*. Elyse Melman was more Ann's friend than hers, but Perri had called her in New York and established a festival rationale.

The next night, after a day spent skiing, Perri arrived at the Egypt Theatre for Larry's screening. She was dressed inconspicuously in black pants and a black silk blouse. She didn't want Larry to see her before she saw him and where he was sitting and whether or not he was with a woman, so Perri had slicked down her hair under a turban and worn a pair of heart-shaped lavender-tinted glasses. It was such a

good disguise, she had scarcely recognized herself in the ladies' room mirror.

Larry wasn't in the theater yet as far as she could see. The
place was two-thirds full: not bad for a documentary program. The lights dimmed halfway, and the audience became
quiet. Then a woman from the festival committee introduced Lawrence Mercator to the audience.

Larry walked out from the wings, his earring gleaming. He
said some introductory words and left the stage by the stairs.
He walked back several rows and sat near—Perri craned her
neck. Larry sat down between two men, one of whom
seemed to be his friend. No, both of them. Great! Fantastic!
She removed the heart-shaped glasses and watched the film.

As the lights came back on, Perri put on her sunglasses
again. The couple in front of Perri stood up and left, and
she sank a little lower in her seat. Then she slipped out of
the auditorium. She put on her new ski jacket and waited
in the shadows by the exterior door. She wasn't sure what
she was going to do, but she felt unable to approach Larry
yet.

Ten minutes later, Larry and his friends came out of the
theater. Perri followed the group up the block, past her
rented car, and along the next block. They reached the Mermaid restaurant and went inside. Perri loitered in the street
for a couple of minutes. She peered into the café window.
The Mermaid had a little bar up front and a dozen tables
toward the rear.

When Perri walked into the restaurant, she saw that Larry
and his friends were sitting three tables in. Larry had his
back to her. One of his friends, a blond man of about thirty,
was facing her, looking at her. She took off her ski jacket
and hung it on a hook. She opened the top two buttons of
her blouse and sat down at the bar. She glanced back at the
table again. The blond man was still looking at her. She gave
him a small, shy smile and turned away on her barstool. This

was going to be a cinch. She couldn't believe her good luck. She ordered a glass of wine, rotated half a turn on her barstool, then got up and went to the back to make a phone call to no one. She averted her face from the group at Larry's table, but knew she was being observed.

When she returned to her barstool, a glass of wine was waiting. "Compliments of that gentleman over there," said the bartender.

Perri looked toward Larry's table. Her blond admirer held up his glass and smiled at her. She held up her glass and smiled back. He said, and mimed in case she didn't hear, "Come here."

She shook her head.

"Come on."

Perri got off her barstool and crossed the room. The blond man took the coats off the empty chair at his table, and Perri sat down and turned away from him. She said to the man at her right, "Hello, Larry."

Larry gave a spasm of surprise. "*Perri?* What are you . . . ?"

"You *said* it was a good festival . . ." she teased.

"That's *it?*"

"Well, there's a little more," Perri said, feigning reluctance. "A friend of mine made a movie that's being shown here, *Family and Friends.* I'm helping with publicity."

"But you never told me." Larry finished his drink and signaled for another.

Perri said, "It was all very last-minute."

The blond friend, miffed, asked, "How do you two know each other?"

Perri said, "We're working together."

The third man said to Larry, "You mean this is the broad you were griping about? Your flako boss lady?" He winked at Perri, who didn't know how many cons the wink covered.

Had Larry really been complaining about her? More than likely. She certainly complained enough about him. . . . But tonight they were away from the office, and she was a little drunk, and for once she felt she had the right line. She said lightly, laughing, "Larry will do anything to hide his secret passion for me."

Larry put down his drink and said with a very small smile, "I guess I even hide it from myself."

"As best you can," Perri said huskily, dramatically. "But you can't hold back passion forever. It just doesn't work."

Ostentatiously, she placed her hand on Larry's leg and gave a squeeze.

"Ooh-ooh," said the blond man, shaking his head in envy. The third man gave a whistle.

Larry looked down at her hand on his leg. Then he put his hand on top of hers and pressed down. He said, "Whatever you say, boss."

They sat like that until dinner came. Perri was silent. She felt her heart bruising her chest. The waiter laid down their plates, and then she had to fake eating. She had to fake heavy flirting for the dragon-lady show she was putting on for Larry's friends. Later, with Larry's hand on her leg, she had to fake watching a movie. And after the movie was over, she had to fake nonchalance when Larry asked if her place had a hot tub.

They didn't make it to the hot tub or even to the bed. As soon as she closed the door of the condo behind them, he reached for her, she grabbed him. Their mouths met hungrily, pushing, mashing. They fell onto the pale blue wall-to-wall carpeting. They pressed against each other tumbling and rolling. Shameless beasts, unable to wait another few seconds, Perri told herelf. But then she thought guiltily, It's *Larry*—why must you fantasize *now*? Or *is* it a fantasy, when I tell myself what's sort of going on.

Meanwhile, Larry was below her, stretched out on the carpet, and she brought both his hands above his head and held them there against the rug. She leaned over his face so her breasts, beneath her blouse, brushed against his cheeks. He sighed and moved his mouth back and forth against the silk. Then they turned over and did it in reverse: he held her hands as if they were bound. His free hand went beneath her jacket to undo her blouse. Then he was browsing beneath, learning her feel and response here and there. They were kissing all the while, and she was finding out what he was like and showing him what she could do. Discovery and exhibition: making love with someone new. The special thrill of sex with someone new you know well: how sex extends the other knowledge, reveals the person from another angle. . . .

She would never have guessed that Larry would be more aroused by rubbing and tickling her under the arms than by petting her breasts—nor would she have imagined her own intense excitement when he pressed his thumbs into her armpits. Almost for spite, to get even, Perri began mouthing his ear, the one with the earring, and now he began breathing fast. When she put in her tongue, he made a whimpering sound and tried to pull away. She held his head tightly against her mouth and sucked on his earlobe. She could feel the gold stud in her mouth, against her tongue, and she heard herself sigh. Larry brought his body hard against hers and began rubbing himself rhythmically against her very middle. It was getting sweeter and sweeter, like high school but better, no battle, just this warm ache, this yearning arc, this . . .

Perri opened her eyes and tried to multiply thirteen by thirteen. But it was too late, her body was surging and soaring, she tried to stay relatively still. Perhaps he wouldn't know. He gave her a few seconds. Then he said in the cranky voice she knew so well, "Didja have a good time?" And she almost came again.

"Well?" he demanded.

Perri felt one final quang between her legs. She said cautiously, "Fair."

"Good," he said, " 'cause I'm just getting started."

They still hadn't removed any of their clothes, although Perri's jacket and blouse were open. She got up and walked across the room. She took off her jacket. Then she sat down on the edge of the bed and pulled off her boots. Larry joined her, boots off, shirt open, belt unbuckled. His pants were unsnapped and unzipped. She began opening her own pants. He said, "Never mind," and pushed her down on the bed. He kneeled over her and thrust his hips forward. He said, "Take it out."

She wanted to tease him for a while with her fingers. But without even pulling his pants all the way down, he rudely stuffed himself into her mouth. She did his bidding. Soon he moaned on the brink, and she pulled her lips away. He jammed himself once or twice into her neck, against her chin, and spurted onto her hair and her blouse.

She let him lie against her for a few minutes. But when she felt her shoulder getting numb under his weight, she eased out from under him. He had fallen into a doze, although she herself was very much awake. She watched him sleeping. She had never seen his face in repose before, and she saw a new gentleness there. Asleep, he looked something like a child. She pulled a blanket over him and turned off the overhead light.

She crossed the room and sat in the kitchen area. It was one thirty-five. She should be sleepy, after a day on the slopes and an evening of tension and fulfillment. But Perri was restless. She realized that she hadn't smoked dope in over twelve hours. No wonder she couldn't get to sleep. She glanced at Larry, asleep across the room although they hadn't even fucked yet. It didn't look like it was going to happen for a while.

When she went to bed with someone for the first time,

Perri liked to be drunk and not stoned—hot and crude and not at all mental. But since intercourse didn't seem imminent, she made herself a midsized joint of her ordinary, workaday grass. Workaday/playanight grass, Perri thought. An herbal nightcap for my nerves. Otherwise, I might be up for hours.

She opened the sliding glass door and stepped out onto a small balcony. She lit her joint and leaned on the rail. A fingernail moon shone lemon over the mountains. Long gray clouds lay furry near the mountain peaks. She began to feel calmer. After all, the gamble had paid off. She had him in her bed. She was spending the night with Larry Mercator— although getting stoned while he slept had not been part of her plans. She tossed the roach over the railing. Perri Ganjaseed.

She went inside and took off her clothes. How would she explain her blouse to the dry cleaners? Would she need to? Was there a different solvent for milk, say, than for sperm? Was it worth the embarrassment to save a favorite blouse? She took off her underpants with regret, for Larry hadn't even seen them. They were a new pair, pink, with tiny satin ribbons, but they were too slimy to put on again. Sex was so messy. Had she been God, she would have designed, divined, *devised* something more aesthetic. And maybe more ecstatic. Like a ten-minute orgasm. How would that have changed world history? At all?

Perri rolled back the hot-tub cover. Chlorine-scented steam billowed into the room. She stepped into the very hot water and sat down on the underwater seat. She didn't turn on the water jets or bubbler, out of deference to Larry. She looked across the room at him and thought: my sleeping lover. Or aren't we lovers till we fuck? Why is intercourse always considered the supreme act between a man and a woman? Because it is best? Because it is trickiest? Because it has, potentially, the greatest consequence?

She closed her eyes and extended her limbs in the water. She was half afloat, half asleep, when the bath became fizzy like soda. The bubbler was on, and Larry stepped into the hot tub.

"Aiieee," he said, lowering himself into the water. "So hot!" He sat down opposite her and stretched out his legs. His toe nudged her breast. He said, "How are ya?"

"I'm pretty good."

"You're pretty stoned," he said. "Your eyes are all red."

"You found me out."

"Got any more?"

"Of course. I'll get it." She stepped out of the tub, tucked a towel around her torso, and went to roll a joint.

He said, "I don't usually use grass."

She said, "I do."

"How often?"

"Couple times a day." This was true if you defined "couple" liberally.

He said, "I've smelled it on your breath."

She said, "I use mints most of the time."

"I know that too." He turned off the bubbler, then turned on the jets. She returned to the hot tub with a lit joint, which she passed to Larry. He inhaled and passed it to her.

To be companionable, she joined him. Soon he said, "I can feel it already. How can you *work* high like this?"

She said, "A) Since I smoke quite a lot I don't feel it that much, and B), I don't often use it for work—only for certain things. Not for being persuasive on the phone, but for creativity, for answers to an impasse, for ideas . . . You have to admit, it's good for ideas."

"I admit nothing," he said, putting the dead joint into the ashtray. "But it's sometimes a good pleasure drug." Then he came toward her. They rubbed against each other in the water. Their arms and legs and mouths were busy. And again there was this competitive edge, this "I'll show you" aspect to their play. She murmured, while rhythmically mouthing his neck, "Take this and this and this."

He said, "Take this," and tried to get inside her.

She pushed him off and said, "Wait."

"Wait? After you hijacked me into your hot tub?"

"You didn't put up much resistance. Anyway, I didn't say no, I said, 'Wait.' Go put on a condom."

He said, "I don't have one."

She said, "I do." Once again Perri left the hot tub, hoping he would follow her. Hot tubs were good for foreplay, she thought, but she didn't like to fuck in the water. Oddly, she felt drier then, less sexy. And she was already very dry from the grass. But Larry remained in the water, so after she brought him the package, she felt she had little choice but to join him in the bath again.

"You travel with condoms," he observed.

"On occasion."

"Pretty sure you'd get me?"

"Well." She thought of her various travels and said mildly, "It just makes sense to have them around."

"If you sleep around."

"Well, I don't. Not anymore. But what's the big deal? Women buy sixty percent of all rubbers sold."

"You sound like a condom ad."

"Well, it's common knowledge. Condom knowledge." She giggled. He didn't.

He said, "You're so superior."

She said, "I'll take that as a compliment."

"You would." He was very erect as he put on the rubber. She could hardly refuse him then, although somehow she wasn't aroused. He had trouble getting into her: the water had washed off her natural lubrication. And her mind was all aprickle, not the way she liked to be (mindless, burning) during sex. He pulled her down upon his lap again. She moved her leg up—and suddenly he was all the way in. She'd been more aroused when he'd accidentally touched her arm in the editing room. But thinking of her yearning then, of her emotional abjection, Perri began to get interested. Slowly she moved up and down. He might ask her again if she'd had a good time. She shimmied her hips against him. He pulled her buttocks hard. "Ohhh," he groaned.

After a bit, he slipped out of her.

She teased, "Didja have a good time?"

He said, "What about you?"

"Sure. But I can never come in water."

"We're getting all waterlogged anyway." He stood up, a dripping pillar.

She said, "You're so skinny."

"You too. Except for these." He dried her with a towel. "This is nicely rounded too," he said, his hand on her behind.

When they were both dry, they lay back on the bed. His index finger moved slowly on her in a single stroke, from the tip of her nose down her lips across her chin and neck then between her breasts across her belly, down, inexorably down. His hand stayed there and established a rhythm.

So he was a gentleman, he wouldn't leave her all alone aroused . . . though considering an earlier round, *perfect* etiquette decreed cunnilingus. Imagining his mouth, she came abruptly on his palm. He pressed back against her. Then he patted her thigh and sat up. He swung his legs over the side of the bed and went to the bathroom.

Perri put on her nightgown and pulled down the bedspread. She got into bed. Waiting for Larry to join her, she fell into a doze, but when she felt him getting into bed, she awoke. She lay still to see what he would do. He lay down on his side of the bed, facing away from her, without touching her at all. He fell asleep almost at once. Perri, piqued, was awake for another half hour. With even the most casual encounter, she liked to lie entwined through the night. But these days there were no casual encounters.

At least she knew Larry well. She moved over to him, snuggled against his back, put her arm around his shoulder. He shook her off him and moved to the very edge of the bed. He liked to sleep alone, untouched, inviolate. She was disappointed but not surprised.

They fucked again in the morning, and that time, by imagining three men watching, Perri came okay with Larry hard inside her. After his own silent orgasm, which followed hers by a minute or two, Larry got out of bed and began putting on his clothes.

Perri said, "It's only seven-thirty."

"The ski lift starts at nine. And I've got to get back to my place and get on my ski clothes and have breakfast and rent skis . . ."

"Well, if you don't want to miss any skiing . . ."

"I don't," Larry said. "The ticket's too expensive."

"Want to meet over there?"

"This morning I'm taking a lesson."

"And lunch?" Was this being pushy? But she felt so sad at his leaving—even though it hadn't been, *especially* because it hadn't been, a night of the most perfect bliss. And now he didn't want to have lunch with her. Perri turned away from him and lifted up her chin. It did no good to feel sad about these things, none at all. But how else could she feel when the seconds ticked away and Larry said nothing?

She wasn't the boss anymore.

Then Larry said, "We could meet at the midstation barbecue place around one."

"Yeah? Okay!" She grinned at him from the bed. Larry left, striding out into the morning.

Perri stayed in bed and put her head under the sheet to

inhale deeply. She thought of what she and Larry had done together in the last eight hours: the flavor and dynamic of each sexual act. The first thing had been really great—when they were just rolling on the floor in all their clothes and she simply couldn't stop herself. Surely, surely, that had been best, Larry in her arms at last, and against her very center. Thinking of it, she was getting hot again. Sex was like dope: when you had it good you wanted more and more—if, that is, you were really obsessive. Perri lingered on in bed another hour.

Yearning at Yaddo,
or,
Achieving Parnassus

S UZANNE CAME TO YADDO TO START a new novel and have an affair. She had written four novels before, none published, but this new one she was about to begin was brimming with promise for her. The fact that she always felt this way when she began a book did not diminish her extravagant hopes for her new novel. *This* would be the story that would make people weep; this the book that would astonish critics and put her on the literary map! At Yaddo, an artists' retreat in upstate New York, she'd have hours and hours each day to spend on her novel—and day after day without domestic duties or interruptions by the kids.

Then, at night, she'd go off with her lover to his room.

That was her Yaddo plan. She'd been married fifteen years and had never been unfaithful to Dave—in part for lack of opportunity. Never before had she spent a night away from her husband and family; never had she followed through on the various party flirtations she'd begun. Surely after all this time she deserved an affair! Surely she should get some reward for persevering as a writer in the face of failure.

After twelve years of writing fiction, her Yaddo acceptance was a career high-water mark. Summer admittance was highly competitive, and as she scarcely had writing credits to her name, the committee must have liked her writing sample. Suzanne was as thrilled with the validation as with the invitation. She was slated for two and a half weeks in August.

In July, Suzanne exercised and rubbed lotions into her skin. Mornings, she revised early stories for a thematic collection on motherhood. She held off beginning her new novel, but sometimes she glimpsed its contours forming in her mind. Afternoons, she took her daughters to the beach. Pym was seven and Camilla was ten: her girls, her wonderful girls!

On August first she took them to camp. Suzanne hugged them against her, but they were impatient with her embraces; they wanted to get settled in their cabins and start making friends.

On August second she kissed her husband Dave good-bye. He hadn't wanted her to go to Yaddo; she knew he suspected her motives; he knew her so well, after all. And she knew him. Departing, she held him to her, trying to convey with her touch that no August fling could interfere with her love for him.

She wished she were as sure about Dave's love for her. There were dozens of women in his practice, and now he'd have the chance to know them better if he chose. She reflected on this as she began her trip to Yaddo. Then she turned on the radio. She heard an old Billy Joel song, "The Stranger," and she sang along with it. It was a golden summer's day and she was off to writers' heaven. Four years earlier, she had written a short story about a harassed mother of five who arranges to go to prison so that she can write her book. Now, instead of going to prison, Suzanne was going to Yaddo.

When she arrived at the estate, a kindly older lady in the office welcomed her and asked if she was tired and how long had it taken her to get to Yaddo. Suzanne smiled and said "Twelve years—but it was worth the wait." They strolled outside. Suzanne took in the rolling lawns, the towering trees, the fountains and the flowers. "It's like Parnassus," she said, "playground of the gods." A staff member gave her a tour of the rose garden, the pool, the tennis court, the mansion, and the other guest houses. Yaddo accommodated twenty-five artists at a time, for a modest and voluntary fee. Most of them lived in the mansion; some lived in outbuildings on the property. Suzanne and two other guests lived in a large cabin. She had her own bedroom, dressing room, and bathroom, all small. And she had a charming screened-in porch as a studio.

Suzanne unpacked at once and set up her computer. She was glad she hadn't written any of her new novel yet—although she knew the first sentence. It had come to her that morning when she was driving on the Northway. Now she rolled it around in her mind again and again. She loved this sentence—although she didn't quite know why. She turned on her computer and tapped in the six talismanic words: "He had made a new friend." She gazed at these words burning blue on her screen. She wasn't sure if she should really write this first afternoon or give herself orientation time. Maybe she'd check out the pool, see who was around. But soon the first sentence suggested a second, and Suzanne decided to stay in her study awhile.

By evening she had gotten a good start on her first chapter. Wayne and Sherri lived in a small town and were trapped in a terrible marriage. All their money was invested in a gas station and country store that they ran together. Sherri had just found out about Wayne's girlfriend, Lucille.

Dinner was the time to meet the other residents and time for Suzanne to pursue the second part of her Yaddo plan. The guests gathered for dinner at six-thirty sharp in the mansion's dining room. It was a formal room, with a quantity of dark carved wood, enormous silver tureens, and a massive marble fireplace. You served yourself buffet-style and chose your own seat.

Suzanne was suddenly shy. Here she was in a roomful of accomplished writers, painters, sculptors, and composers—all of whom knew each other, none of whom knew her. She didn't know where to sit and hesitated with her plate of food and glass of water, acutely self-conscious in the sumptuous room. The other people, mostly her own age and younger, were talking to one another and seating themselves. She had the sense of there being rather more women than men. At the nearest table, Suzanne saw a skinny fellow who looked interesting, and she sat down next to him. Up close, he had melting brown eyes, a scraggly beard, and an intelligent face. Suzanne thought: a Candidate.

"I'm Lief," he said. "Did you arrive today?"

Suzanne nodded. "I got here this afternoon. I'm still over-whelmed by the beauty of the place."

"I know what you mean," said a pretty woman with white skin and a mass of black ringlets. "I got here yesterday. What will you be doing here?"

"I'm beginning a novel."

"That's brave of you, to start it here."

Suzanne beamed at her.

The woman said in a high, breathy voice, "My name's Jessica. I'm a playwright."

"Nice to meet you." Suzanne wished she liked theater more and could talk intelligently about plays.

Everyone began eating. The food—cold chicken breasts in an intriguing white sauce—was very good. Suzanne looked down the table and did a quick count. Sure enough, her instinct had been right. There were almost two women there for every man. At the other tables, much the same ratio prevailed. This was disheartening, especially as she guessed that several of the male residents were gay. Surely Sean here on her right was gay—an odd, behatted little fellow with bright eyes and pink cheeks. He was dressed entirely in white and he was talking about his novel, "a roman à clef about the art world." He was one of her housemates. Jade, a sculptor sitting at the head of the table, was her other housemate—and, as it turned out, she was gay too.

There were only a few possibilities for Suzanne, and of those few, she thought, no doubt some were already taken. She looked into Lief's eyes with real attention. "Tell me about your project here," she said. Lief told her he was a folklorist writing a study of Oswego County. Suzanne asked him some questions about his work. Then she wondered aloud, "What *is* in this chicken? It's so good."

"It's chicken tonnato," said Lief.

"With *tuna fish?*" asked Suzanne—in disbelief and disappointment. She took another forkful. It no longer tasted nearly as good now that she knew the secret ingredient.

After dinner, the group went outside and sat on the broad stone terrace that overlooked the fountain. Suzanne thought that even a few years earlier there would have been cigarettes and wine. Now, in the abstemious nineties, people murmured to each other politely, then drifted off to their studios. "Back to work," said Lief as he wandered away.

He was a frail fellow, she observed, watching him recede into the night. She thought that what he needed (although he probably didn't know it) was some generous, earthmother type. She imagined being in bed with him. She would warm him up, set him free. His thin body would tremble against hers: his nerves would be next to the surface. He would clutch her to him in rapture and disbelief. He would mutter, "Never before, it's never been like this for me." And she would hug him hard.

She had never been to bed with someone lighter than herself, and inflicting her will and her weight might be interesting. Was that why some women slept with each other? Suzanne wished she could drum up a sexual interest in women—at least during her stay at Yaddo, where there were probably more gay women than straight men.

Two days later, once again on the terrace after dinner, not drinking and not smoking with the other guests, Suzanne looked around and concluded that besides Lief, there were only two Candidates. There was Archibald, a tall, distinguished-looking playwright in his fifties, recently divorced, and Chuck, a stocky poet in his early thirties, single, with blond hair and small, pale aquamarine eyes. Chuck was a little too young and a little too heavy for her, but she found him very sexy.

As if she had sent him a signal, he came over to her and said, so that others could hear, "How do you stay in such great shape? It's hard to believe you're the mother of two." He added, "I didn't mean that in a bad way."

If there hadn't been people around, she would have replied teasingly, "Why not?"

Chuck continued. "Do you do a lot of exercise?" He himself was wearing a green tank top that exposed his upper arms. She decided that if he was exposing them this way, they must be muscular and not fat, as she had thought. It was hard to tell; night was falling.

They discussed their exercise routines for a while. Then he looked at his watch and said vaguely, "I have to get back."

Suzanne returned to the cabin to find Jade doing push-ups on the living room floor. Jade explained, "This gives me energy for my evening jolt." The notion of working after dinner continued to dismay Suzanne. Surely with visitors forbidden in the studios between nine and four (artists were given a lunch pail at breakfast), and no communal meal until six-thirty, there was enough time to work during the day.

More than enough! At home Suzanne worked for two or three hours. Then she'd pick up her daughters from school or put on a load of wash, or do the marketing. Here, she had no domestic duties whatsoever. She was amazed at how many hours there were until dinner. She missed Dave and the girls, but during her first week at Yaddo she doubled and tripled her usual number of pages per day.

Things with Lief weren't advancing as quickly: he was always chatty with her, yet remote. They hadn't yet spent any time alone together. On the fifth day, at dinner, Lief sat at another table instead of sitting near her, although the place to her left was empty. A young woman called June, who had arrived that afternoon, sat down next to Suzanne. June was in her twenties. She looked like a modest Mariel Hemingway. This stay at Yaddo was pursuading Suzanne that artists were better-looking than most people. Yet no one was getting it on!

Or were they? Had AIDS really changed the social scene here? Or were lovers just being very discreet? A few of the guests were married, after all—although Suzanne was the only mother, she had learned. On her second night at Yaddo, sitting at the long table, she had talked exultantly about her daughters. Impulsively, she had even passed their photographs around the table. Now she was sorry she had erected this fence between her and the other guests. She was married, a mother, respectable—or so they thought.

For although she had the most conventional lifestyle of all the artists here (she actually lived in the suburbs and drove a minivan), Suzanne thought that she probably had the most subversive heart. The dinner conversations tended to be tepid unless she rolled a few grenades. The night she said, with only small exaggeration, that unconscious motivation was not a useful concept for her, she outraged everybody at her table, even Chuck.

Also, as far as she knew, she was the only doper in the place—but it could be that people were holding and hiding. The Yaddo information sheet included the following warning: "The use of and/or possession of *marijuana* or other drugs *prohibited by law* is also prohibited at Yaddo, and anyone who has or uses drugs here will be asked to leave at once." This meant to Suzanne that she shouldn't talk about grass with the other artists or smoke in her studio or bedroom—only in the woods. She took inspiration walks twice a day on an overgrown trail that led off through the trees near the cabin. Marijuana was part of her process, and no artists' colony was going to change that.

On the sixth night, once again Lief sat at a different table from hers, and Suzanne decided he definitely wasn't interested in her. She faced left to talk to Archibald Delaney. Archibald was fifty-five, southern, and charming. Wouldn't an older man be fun! Tender, experienced, grateful! Archibald's full head of silver hair was combed straight back, and he looked very handsome tonight. She held out one conversational morsel after another, and he responded with mild interest. Then he got a phone call and was gone.

Sex with Archibald Delaney would be the opposite of sex with Lief. She would be the innocent, the learner, the precocious evil child. He would be older and superior: she would eagerly abase herself for him. Since he was in his fiftes, he might be hard to arouse, but he would surely teach her how. And she would be his love slave, giving pleasure on command, abject for his approval. This was the fantasy into which she'd fit his actual being, his smell, his tech-

SKIN

nique, his passion, his southern accent. She wondered who had called him on the phone.

Suzanne wandered outside the mansion. There was nothing to do but go to her cabin. But while her novel was going well during the day, she didn't want to work on it at night. After all, she'd already spent six hours on it. She wasn't a writing machine, dammit, she was a human being.

Ahead of her, she saw two figures in the darkness, going off down the path. It was that lovely dark-haired Jessica, walking beside Jim, a married composer. Watching them, Suzanne felt a pang of real longing. Why wasn't she able to connect here? It wasn't just a question of sex, it was a matter of intimacy—she wasn't making any friends. Hell, she hadn't even found a tennis partner.

Jessica turned around. "Suzanne? Is that you?"

"It's me." Suzanne caught up with them.

Jessica said, "Jim's going to play me some of his music in the tower. Do you want to join us?"

"I'd love to." She felt like weeping with gratitude. She added, "But I can't stay long." She said this so Jim would know she wasn't going to spoil any seduction plans he might have for Jessica.

Jim's lodgings were off in the woods by a lake. Yaddo guests eagerly visited one another's quarters and studios to see the other possibilities available and to assess where each stood in the Yaddo pecking order.

Jim had a beautiful work space: a round and airy tower with a piano and a Franklin stove. He said bats sometimes flew in at night; Suzanne hoped to see one.

Jim played Suzanne and Jessica a tape of the piece he was composing here at Yaddo. It was unlike anything Suzanne had ever heard: an exuberant synthesis of classical music and Brazilian dance tunes. Occasionally Jim would play the piano along with the tape. Jessica closed her eyes and smiled in happy concentration.

When the tape ended, Suzanne jumped up. "Thank you," she said. "That was wonderful. I've got to go."

"Where are you running off to?" asked Jessica.

Suzanne said, "I must go back to work."

Jim said, "You jumped up like there was a bomb in your chair!"

"Oh, no, I just got this . . . impulse. I'll see you at breakfast."

Walking back along the dark path, she wondered if she would indeed see Jessica and Jim at breakfast the next morning, or if they would satiate themselves time and again until noon. For Jessica's sake, she wished Jim were single.

Sexual attraction was a mystery. She supposed Jim was handsomer than Chuck, but Jim had never been a Candidate for her.

She smoked a joint on the way back to the cabin. When she reached her studio, she knew she didn't want to work on her novel. She had put Wayne and Sherri to sleep for the night—under different roofs. No—a short story was just beginning to crystallize for her, and she sat down to watch it. She saw that for this story she would scarcely need to invent a thing: her tasks would be to simplify and shape, describe and dramatize.

She opened a new computer file.

The first three pages wrote themselves.

Oh, she was a very bad person to be writing this one! This story, unlike her new novel, was guaranteed to be personally embarrassing—even humiliating. This one would neither sell to the slicks nor get taken by a quarterly. And it would infuriate Dave—if he ever saw it. There was no reason at all to keep writing this—except she had to see where it would go. Suzanne knew the ending would be there and that it would show itself after a while. She stayed up till two and missed breakfast, so she didn't find out if Jessica and Jim had missed it too.

SKIN

At five that afternoon she had a tennis game scheduled with Roy Blynker, a very young, very tall, very successful short story writer. He was waiting for her at the court when she arrived. The court was taken by June and Lanie, a painter who was clearly the better player of the two. "We'll be another few minutes," Lanie said. Watching, Suzanne thought Lanie would be a good partner for her. Finally, Lanie and June were finished.

June said, "I have to go shower."

Lanie said, "See you tomorrow." Then, to Suzanne and Roy: "Mind if I watch?"

"Not at all," said Suzanne. She played better in front of an audience, and this would be, she sensed, an audition to play with Lanie. She usually preferred playing tennis with a woman than playing with a man: men got so bitter when they lost.

Roy, it turned out, was not a good player. He had, of course, power, and he covered the court well, but he hit most balls out and into the net. It was maddening not being able to establish a rhythm in a rally and irritating to hold back on her shots because she didn't want to make him look bad in front of Lanie. After ten minutes Lanie left, and Suzanne worked on improving her backhand. She began to get into her game. At the end of the hour she said, to be polite, "That was fun." Roy didn't say anything.

Suzanne took a shower and dressed carefully for dinner in a rose-colored tank top and white jeans. She wore long silver earrings and carried a white sweater.

Entering the dining room in that crucial minute after six-thirty (people here were insanely prompt), Suzanne saw where Archibald was sitting and planted her sweater on the chair next to his. "Hello," she said, "mind?"

"My pleasure, Suzanne," he said in his courtly southern way.

"I wanted to ask you something about *By God*," she said

when she returned with her plate of food. She had borrowed one of Archibald's plays from the Yaddo Authors Library and had read it in bed the night before.

He didn't seem surprised that she had read his play, and when she posed her question, he answered her at length. Then she asked, "What are you working on now?"

"A play about Colette."

"Great material," said Suzanne. "I've always wanted someone to lock me in my room and make me write." She let this hang awhile, but Archibald did not ask about her personal life. Suzanne continued. "At this point, are you writing or researching?"

"Both," said Archibald. "I'm rereading Colette's book *The Pure and the Impure.* Have you read it?"

Suzanne shook her head.

"It's brilliant," said Archibald. "Incredibly wise. Nobody understands bisexuality like Colette."

Uh-huh. Suzanne nodded dumbly. Too bad! Because for Archibald to assess Colette's wisdom on the subject implied an expertise of his own, and this knowledge, while it might have made him more interesting to her ten years ago, *today* meant that Archibald was at once and decisively Not a Candidate.

And he wanted her to know it. That hurt Suzanne's pride. She swallowed and said, "My favorite book of Colette's is *Claudine at School,* which I read at far too young an age."

After dinner she returned to the cabin and removed her silver earrings. Then she found herself moving toward the studio. Once again she had worked on the novel during the day; now she opened the file on her rogue story. It called to her like a lover in the night.

A lover in the night! She had been here long enough to see that it might not happen after all. These were the nineties, she kept reminding herself. And she was a mother, taboo.

She preferred to think that sexual mores had changed than to consider the alternative: that she had lost her pull as an attractive woman.

The next afternoon at the pool, Suzanne and Jessica talked about the Yaddo men. "I was told it would be like this," said Jessica. "Slim pickings."

"Jim is nice," said Suzanne.

"And married. He said he had 'special feelings' for me and was very 'confused.' But I don't want another affair with a married man. Is *anyone* making it here, do you think?"

Suzanne said, "Where are the wild-eyed artists of yester-year?"

That night again Suzanne worked on her story. Then she went into the kitchen.

Sean, wearing white as usual, was making herbal tea. "Would you like any?" he asked her.

"Thank you. That would be nice."

"Ever since I got sick, I've been drinking herbal tea before bed."

"How long have you been sick?" asked Suzanne, hoping they weren't talking about what she suddenly knew they were.

"About four years. I shouldn't be alive," Sean said cheer-fully. "They can't seem to find any T-cells!"

"But you're feeling okay at the moment?"

"Oh, fine. For now."

"Gee." What do you say? He handed her a cup of tea. She took a sip and said, "It's delicious."

Sean said, "I was wondering. Are you interested in going into town tomorrow night to hear *The Art of Fugue*? I have an extra ticket, and I could use a glamorous date."

Suzanne looked at him, surprised. So she was glamorous to somebody!

Then he said, "Come on, mom."

"I'm not *your* mom," said Suzanne, "but sure, that would be fun."

The next afternoon, on the telephone with Dave, Suzanne mentioned that she was going to a concert that night, and he snapped, "Who are you going with?"

"Dave, even you couldn't be jealous of Sean." She told her husband a little about him. "I realize he's the first person I've known who has AIDS. Isn't that odd? Aren't we sheltered?"

Dave said, "Thank God we're somewhat sheltered from that."

Somewhat! Did that mean *he* was having an affair? Wouldn't that be an irony!

After dinner Suzanne changed into a short black and white dress and red high heels. "Snazzy," said Sean. After the concert they had a snack at a Victorian hotel in the center of town. "Do you think I can make Roy fall in love with me?" asked Sean with a grin.

"Roy's awfully young," Suzanne said, "and he even acts like a child. He won't even talk to me since we played tennis together and I played better than he did."

"He's such a cutie though," said Sean. He pushed his plate away. Suzanne noticed that there were thick crusts of his roast beef and arugula sandwich just sitting there about to be discarded. She herself was still hungry after her fruit salad, and she picked up one of Sean's crusts and ate it.

Sean looked at Suzanne, seemingly surprised. She was surprised at his surprise. They were no longer on campus—they could dispense with the Yaddo gentility for the time being. In the real world, friends ate from each other's plates.

Unless one of them had AIDS. As Suzanne reached for another crust, her hand stopped midair.

Sean said gently, "You just remembered."

She nodded, blushing.

He said, "I'm glad you forgot. And it's perfectly safe."

"Of course." But they both knew she wouldn't eat the second crust.

He said, "I forget, myself, when I'm writing. That's why it's so good to be here."

"Have you ever written as much?"

"Never. Never in my life."

The next day at breakfast, Lanie asked to play tennis with Suzanne the following day.

After breakfast Suzanne brought her lunchbox back to her cabin and took her inspiration walk. Then she sat down at her computer. Contemplating the next pages of her novel, a wave of overwhelming grief rolled over her. She hid her face in her hands and huddled against herself, rocking slightly. She blew her nose. This was ridiculous. Wayne and Sherri were furious at each other, but they weren't really suffering yet. Not the way they would hurt in Chapters 4 and 5.

That afternoon Suzanne finished Chapter 2, and she wore her skimpy peach shirt to dinner to celebrate. Chuck came over to her when she was serving herself salad at the side table. He looked very tan and sensuous, golden in a yellow shirt. He murmured to her, "You're looking sexy tonight." Three other people were listening, so she could not say "So are you" and she could not say "It must be frustration." Never had she gone so long without at least a cuddle!

Before she could think of what to say to Chuck, he went to sit by Lanie. There were no seats at their table.

Suzanne once again didn't know where to sit. Jessica's table was also full. She sat at the empty half of the long middle table, her least-favorite place. To her surprise, Lief sat down next to her. He gripped her arm. "Suzanne," he said. "I've just heard the most disturbing news."

"What?" She hadn't been touched in so long, her arm tingled.

"A very good friend of mine is having an affair."

Suzanne looked at him, waiting.

Lief said. "He has a child! And a wonderful wife! Oh, it's so horrible. Do you think I should tell her?"

"Of course not! You can't meddle in their marriage."

"You're right. But I'm so upset by all this."

"It doesn't have to break up their marriage, you know."

"But it's wrong! I'm shocked at him. Shocked!"

"Lief," Suzanne said, "you sound so old-fashioned."

"Perhaps I am!"

"No sex outside of marriage?" she teased softly. "Or before? Not even for you?" Lief had never been married.

"That's the right way," said Lief. "Don't you honestly think so?"

"No, Lief, I honestly don't. I believe in passion before, during, and after marriage. I believe in it for the older and younger and middle generations. And I don't think extramarital sex always leads to disaster."

Suzanne smiled to see that she had made Lief blush. She said, "Why don't you show me your studio?" She saw him get flustered, so she took pity on him. "Come on, Jessica and I were just saying we've never been in any of the Courtyard Studios. Give us a tour."

At Jessica's name, he brightened up. After dinner he showed them his studio. Suzanne found it cheering that his was the darkest and dankest she'd yet seen. Then the three of them went to the movies in Suzanne's minivan. On the way to town Lief told them he had no intention of paying the voluntary fee Yaddo asked. "I can't afford it," he said.

On the way back he let it slip that he was buying a Stephen Crane first edition for five hundred dollars.

"The great moralist," Suzanne sneered to Jessica after they had dropped Lief off at the Courtyard. "Takes advantage of Yaddo and invests the money instead. He told me tonight that he doesn't believe in sex outside of marriage."

"I'm not surprised. He's one of those Puritan types. You can spot them a mile away."

"I can't," said Suzanne, "but I haven't been in circulation for a while."

"Are you in circulation here?" asked Jessica.

Suzanne said, "Apparently not."

The next afternoon she was scheduled to play tennis with Lanie at four. It had rained in the morning, and at three forty-five it began to drizzle again. Suzanne was sure their game would be canceled. At four-fifteen there was no sign of Lanie, so Suzanne put on her raincoat and went on an inspiration walk. She always took the same route and sat on the same tree stump in the forest to smoke her joint. She finished her joint, squirted drops in her eyes to cut down on the red, and began sucking a mint. Then she started back. When she entered the cabin, Suzanne saw Lanie in the living room, in full tennis gear. "Well," said Lanie. "Aren't we going to play?" Lanie was thirty, with short blond hair and big brown eyes. The headband she wore for athletics made her face look round. Her body went straight up and down without indenting at the waist.

Suzanne said, "Isn't it a little wet out?"

"Not really. It's stopped raining now, and there are just two puddles on the court. We'll use old balls. Come on, I need the exercise."

"Uh." Suzanne never liked to be physically active when she was stoned, but she knew Lanie would be mad with her if they didn't play. "All right. Let me make some coffee and get less, uh, dreamy. I was all set to write. I thought our game was off."

She changed into her shorts and bolted down a cup of coffee. They walked to the court. As she was unzipping her racket, Suzanne almost said, "Lanie, I might not play my best, I just smoked a joint." Then she thought it wouldn't be a sporting thing to say. It excused her performance in advance.

As soon as she began to play, Suzanne saw that her timing and coordination were off. But all too soon Lanie said, "Shall we play a set?"

Suzanne lost three-six. She thought it was a wonder she got any games at all. Lanie seemed well pleased with the encounter and suggested that they play every morning it was clear.

That night after dinner she sat on the wide stone railing next to Chuck. He said, "I hear you and Lanie played tennis."

"Hot gossip," said Suzanne with a smile. "Actually, I didn't play my best." She said, as if jock to jock, "I was, you might say, chemically challenged."

"Really?" He was looking at her with interest and surprise. She was getting just the effect she wanted.

"Yeah," said Suzanne. "It was raining, so I smoked a joint to get back to work and I was really stoned when she appeared ready to play."

"Chuck!" said Lanie. "We've been looking for you. Come on."

"See you," he said to Suzanne. He explained apologetically, "I've got this poker game."

"Have fun." She didn't like poker, but she was hurt they hadn't asked her to join them.

She dreamed of Chuck that night, dreamed he was squeezing her hands, utterly inflaming her just by gripping her fingers.

The next morning it was pouring. That night Chuck and June were reading together at eight o'clock.

Suzanne entered the lounge at eight o'two to find Chuck in the middle of reading a poem. She sat down as quietly as she could in the last chair in the room. Chuck recited his lyrics in so soft a voice, she had to strain to hear: she thought it was a performance choice of thrilling self-confidence. He was inspired by Mediterranean islands and cathedrals. His poems were delicate and fragile, like smoke.

You could never know by a man's appearance what his art would be like—just as you could never really tell what he'd be like in bed, although you might have woven fantasies about him. Listening to Chuck read in his soft, deep voice, Suzanne knew in her head and in her heart and in her groin that he wasn't just a Candidate, he was the One. Lief and Archibald had just been diversions; it was Chuck she had craved from the start.

God, she was lonely here at Yaddo! She missed her family, she missed her friends; she missed intimacy. When you had an affair, you took off your clothes and removed your constraints. Maybe she had to fuck to be free.

Chuck finished a poem and said abruptly, "That's it." Everybody clapped.

June began reading her story. It was the story of a mother who runs away from her children. Suzanne thought of Pym, who still couldn't tell time. Tears filled her eyes.

When June read the part in her story where the little boys lie to their friends to account for their mother's disappearance, Suzanne's tears spilled over onto her cheeks. What if Camilla began walking in her sleep again? What if Pym, only seven, wasn't really ready for camp?

After all, Suzanne, at forty-one, wasn't having much fun at *her* sleepaway camp. It hadn't proved so easy to find a lover in the night. One way or another, she had been rejected twice.

Seeing Suzanne cry at her story, June looked very pleased.

There were refreshments afterward, provided by Chuck and June: an actual alcoholic punch and pretzels and chips. It was easy for Suzanne to tell June and Chuck that she loved their work.

Chuck was wearing a black T-shirt and white pants. She

saw tonight that one of his front locks was a lighter blond, almost a silver. Why had she never noticed this attractive detail? He said to Suzanne, "You looked so sad during June's story."

"I know. I was."

"Inexplicably moved? For unconscious reasons?"

"Explicably moved. For obvious reasons. Besides, the story's very good."

"You just looked so lonely. Are you lonely?"

Every part of her sighed yes—but how could she admit it to him? Certainly not with Jim and Lanie and Roy all within earshot. She was suddenly angry with Chuck that he flirted with her only publicly. She saw it meant he wasn't serious in his pursuit.

"No," Suzanne said. "I'm not lonely."

If she had been honest, she wondered later, would it have made any difference?

Chuck began talking to Lanie. Without the headband, Lanie looked almost glamorous. She wore a flowing tunic over fitted pants, and you really couldn't tell that she didn't have a waist.

Suzanne found herself face-to-face with Roy. "What did you think of June's story?" she asked.

He shrugged and blinked and turned away.

Jessica came to Suzanne's side. "Come here," she said, tugging her away and into the hallway. "I have to tell you something private. You know about me and Jim. How he said he had 'special feelings' for me and was very confused. And how we decided not to. Because of his wife."

Suzanne nodded absently. She wanted to get back inside and tell Chuck she had lied—she was incredibly lonely at Yaddo. All she had to do was pull him away from the others, as Jessica had done to her, and say, "I have to tell you something private." Why had she never thought of this before?

SKIN

Jessica continued. "Well, this afternoon Jim told June the very same thing. He had 'special feelings' for her and was 'confused.' Can you believe it? He even used the same words."

"Well, he's not a writer."

" 'Special feelings'!"

"Look, you're both lovely women," said Suzanne. "Last week he liked you, but you turned him down. This week he likes June."

"Don't you think that's incredibly shallow?"

"He has to move fast," Suzanne said. "Before he gets back to his spouse. I know the feeling."

"Suzanne!"

"Just kidding."

Suzanne returned to the lounge to find Chuck was gone. She ran down the path to look for him and tell him yes, she was lonely. She might even say that she'd had a sexy dream about him. Because although only hands were involved, it had been very hot.

She rounded a curve and saw him just ahead of her, walking next to Lanie, his hand upon her upper arm.

Too late! Suzanne stopped and watched as they entered the mansion, where he had a room on the third floor: he had shown her his window once. Now, out of sheer masochism, she watched Chuck's window. It was dark. Above the mansion, the stars were out. Tomorrow would be clear and she would show Lanie how she really played tennis. She saw a bright light go on Chuck's room. A moment later, the light dimmed: he must have turned on the bed lamp and turned off the overhead fixture.

He had turned off the overhead light so that they could make love—and he had turned on the bed lamp so that he could watch. If Suzanne were in bed with him now, she thought, he'd be looking at her body. Perhaps he'd admire her taut brown stomach and her smooth white breasts. She

would exult in his bulk, in his smooth taffy skin, in the
delicacy of his hands and the obduracy of his cock. It would
be thick. Making love with Chuck she would keep her eyes
open to take in his meaty body with her soul, to dissolve in
his strange pale eyes.

Suzanne headed home to the cabin. It was too early for
bed, so she lit into her short story, anger and desire fueling
her fingers.

The next morning was sunny. Suzanne dressed for tennis.
Her shorts and shirt fit her well. She wore her turquoise stud
earrings. She was going to whip Lanie on the court. She was
going to get revenge.

But Lanie didn't show up for breakfast, and neither did
Chuck. Suzanne lingered on at the table until the last very
minute. She was furious. The rudeness of it! Breaking a tennis date! Flaunting their new affair! But maybe it wasn't
their first night together. Maybe they'd been lovers for days,
or weeks—since before Suzanne's arrival.

When she returned to the cabin, Suzanne wrote long letters to Dave and Camilla and Pym. She had only a few more
days at Yaddo, but she wanted to put down on paper how
much she loved them. She also printed a notice about her
reading. She would read the night before she left. She
walked to the mansion, put her letters in the mail basket,
and taped her notice on the mail table so that everyone
could see it. God knows what she was going to read. Maybe
a story from the motherhood collection. Maybe the first or
second chapters of her new novel.

She took her inspiration walk somewhat later than usual.
On her way back from the stump, she pictured Lanie and
Chuck in bed, both blond, both single, both the same age,
intimate and gossipy after their night of passion. At one
point this morning, Lanie had probably giggled, "Whoops!
I've missed my tennis game with Suzanne."

And Chuck had probably said something like "Hey, did you know she was totally stoned the last time you played?"

At least Lanie would know that—would know how gallant Suzanne had been not to tell her.

Big deal. It wasn't much consolation for not getting Chuck. Thinking of being naked with him, of his beefy, smooth back, of his slow smile and small blue eyes, the heat from her breasts met the heat from her crotch. In ecstasy, would Chuck scream? Would he moan?

When she returned to the cabin, Suzanne did something really depraved. She worked on her short story *in the day*. She justified it as a vacation from her novel, a break from Wayne and Sherri and Lucille. She had found out that some guests here actually took vacation days off work, which she, at least, hadn't done yet. She felt she had to come back with many pages to show Dave, or at least tell him about.

All along, she had been writing her rogue story on faith, certain that she'd come upon the ending sometime. Today, halfway through the piece, she found it.

When Suzanne saw the ending, smiling at her through the mist, she was initially indignant. This would certainly condemn the story to the drawer! For she saw that the story had to curve in on itself—like a fox biting its own tail. And she knew that what she viewed as slyly self-referential, a nod to a grand and witty tradition, could be seen as merely self-indulgent.

Nonetheless, it was the only way to end the thing. If only she could plant an Escher suggestion, as if subliminally, to avert reader indignation at the close . . .

At four o'one precisely, Lanie tapped at the screen of Suzanne's studio. Lanie was all dressed for tennis.

Suzanne said less coldly than she had intended, "I thought we were going to play tennis this morning." She was curious to see what excuse Lanie would summon.

"I didn't feel too well this morning," said Lanie. A blatant lie! She looked radiant! "I missed breakfast."

"I noticed," said Suzanne.

"I'm sorry—there was no way to get in touch with you."

You could have sent Chuck down, Suzanne didn't say.

Lanie said, "Let's play now."

"Oh, all right." Suzanne was still in her tennis things from the morning. She closed the file. This story was getting longer and longer. She grabbed her racket and her balls.

Everything was different this time. Suzanne met the ball early and well. She pounded it where Lanie wasn't. She got off great drop shots and lobs. She won, six-zero, six-one. "I don't understand it," said Lanie.

"You're probably still tired," said Suzanne. "From this morning." Tell Chuck the score, she didn't say.

Alone again in her single bed that night, Suzanne touched herself, and as she went over the top she thought of Chuck and cried out.

She wondered if Sean or Jade had heard.

She wondered if Yaddo had been more fun in the seventies and eighties. But fun wasn't the point here, was it? It was all work and beauty. Didn't anyone except her want to rebel against the damn graciousness here? Certainly the elegance was socially constricting.

The next night, there was a U-2 concert at an amphitheater that adjoined the estate. During the sound checks that afternoon, Suzanne biked down old paths, looking for a back way into the concert. The amphitheater property was surrounded by a chain-link fence topped with barbed wire. But at one point in the woods, a tree had fallen down and bent the barbed wire flat. You could climb over the fence at this point and jump down—although you wouldn't be able to climb back. Presumably, though, you'd leave through the gate with the rest of the crowd. The point was getting in.

Rather, since she never even considered buying a ticket, the point was *breaking* in.

Suzanne asked around a bit after dinner to see if anyone was interested in crashing the concert with her, but nobody was. She didn't want to do it alone, so she abandoned the idea. It would be highly embarrassing to be caught alone climbing over the fence. And at her age too! When would rebellion stop bringing her joy? Surely she was too old to want to carve her name in the long mahogany dining room table or play loud music during quiet hours. She wondered whether her orneriness here was related to her anger at not being able to publish her novels.

Under a quarter moon, Suzanne sat alone by the Yaddo pool and listened to the U-2 concert, although the sound was badly distorted to the bass. She decided she was *not* going to read from her motherhood collection after all. It was just too safe. So what should she read? So far, her new novel was basically "set ups"; the heartbreak and misery lay just ahead. And Suzanne didn't want to read from any of her old novels.

Sean said the next morning, "Read something funny. People love that."

"I never know if it's funny," said Suzanne. "I've been surprised both ways."

Walking back to the cabin in the rain, Suzanne and Sean admired the mushrooms underneath the pine trees. "I think they're morels," said Sean. "But I'm not altogether sure."

"That's the nice thing about writing," said Suzanne. "Mistakes aren't fatal."

Sean said, "What if you die of shame?"

"I'm leaving the morning after my reading—so I can disgrace myself and flee."

"Clever of you to plan it all out."

"I haven't planned it *all* out," she said. "I haven't decided *how* to disgrace myself."

That afternoon Suzanne finished her short story. For about ninety seconds after writing "the end," she felt absolutely elated. She had, after all, snapped the stuff into shape! But then depression hit her. Now that she was finished with the story—what? It was, after all, resolutely noncommercial. Why had she even bothered?

It was a little like sexual desire. You couldn't say why a certain shape and subject drew you on, but you had to follow it anyway. This story had certainly surprised her. She had not intended to work on anything but her small-town novel during her stay here. She'd felt bad to the bone—and alive to the max—while cheating on her novel with her story.

The next morning it was raining again, and the yellow and orange mushrooms in the forest were rigid with vigor, turgid with health. That night was her reading, and she still wasn't sure what she would read. She lay the various possibilities out upon her desk. Her eyes lingered on one.

I dare you, she thought.

Now that she had abandoned all erotic hope, dinnertime was more relaxed for Suzanne. On her last night at Yaddo, she sat next to Jessica. She was sorry she hadn't spent more time with her: they had each placed more importance on men than on each other. "Who's that?" asked Jessica.

Suzanne saw that at the next table there was somebody new. He had curly dark hair and glowing dark eyes. "A new man," said Suzanne. "A painter, I bet." She and Jessica had agreed that visual artists were the best-looking.

As she walked down the long room to get more salad, Suzanne felt the new man's eyes linger on her—or was that just wishful thinking? After dinner, on the stone terrace in front of the Great Hall, Suzanne heard Jessica tell him that there was a reading that night. "I'm really tired from my trip here," he said. "I think I'll just turn in. Who's giving the reading?"

Suzanne, out of shame, moved away. She went back to

the cabin and lay on her bed until it was time to get dressed. Applying her lipstick, she was suddenly scared. She knew what she had dared herself to read.

She took it, and only it, with her, so she wouldn't chicken out at the last minute.

This was the ideal audience to hate this piece, and so she had to read it.

Suzanne walked to the lounge where the readings were held. She chose a seat at one end of the room. She poured herself a glass of water. She looked around the room. Her eyes rested on Lief and on Archibald, on Lanie and on Chuck. Roy, she noticed, had stayed away. The assembled residents waited expectantly: it was 8:01 P.M.

The door opened, and in walked the new man. He had come to her reading despite his fatigue. Maybe it wasn't too late after all!

Suzanne took a sip of water. She looked around the room once more. Chuck made the thumbs-up sign. Jessica gave her a smile. Sean blew her a kiss.

They would never feel the same about her after this.

She took a deep breath. She took out her new story. She began to read: " 'Shannon came to Parnassus to start a new novel and have an affair. She had written four novels before, none published, but this new one she was about to begin was brimming with promise for her. . . . ' "

Green Silk Panties

AFTER TWENTY YEARS OF MARRIAGE, Richard told Audrey he loved someone else. Audrey listened in numb disbelief. For the next three months—in the house and on the phone and in their joint therapy sessions—she wept and raged and begged him to stay.

But Richard left anyway, to start a new life with his girlfriend, Irene. As he took his suitcases downstairs and into his car, Audrey lay facedown on the marriage bed, with pillows over her head, but she still heard his tires crush the gravel in the driveway.

She grieved for another three months. Then a divorced girlfriend asked Audrey to come with her to a local zydeco dance. Audrey began making excuses, but her friend was insistent, so Audrey finally agreed. Richard didn't like to dance, and Audrey did, and perhaps it was time for her to stop suffering. After all, *he* wasn't suffering, was he? The bastard! Audrey had a vague recollection of Dennis Quaid and Ellen Barkin doing zydeco dancing in *The Big Easy*, and she began looking forward to the dance.

On the night of the dance, she was drying her hair when her friend called to say she was coming down with the flu. Audrey was already dressed, so to her own surprise she set off for the dance by herself.

The dance was held in a church basement less than a mile from her house, so Audrey walked instead of driving. She arrived early, to take advantage of the lesson before the dance, but the music was fast and the instruction was confusing, so if somebody asked her to dance, she would just have to learn the moves from him.

When the lesson was over and the band came onstage, the experienced dancers went onto the floor. One young man stood out. He was tall and blond, and he wore a green tank top, from which descended long, muscled arms. He danced well, sending his partners out in intricate breaks and whirls. When he smiled, there were dimples in his cheeks. Watching him dance, Audrey dubbed him "Golden Arms."

She sat and watched the dancers for several numbers, and then, to her intense relief, she was finally asked onto the floor. After that she had many partners: some old, some young, some handsome, some plain. Most danced well, and when it was clear that she did not, they were polite about it, but didn't dance with her again. Luckily, there were others to ask her a first time. Richard had rarely acknowledged that she was good-looking, so Audrey was pleased that at forty-two she could still attract partners.

Between dances she sat on a folding chair. Even dancing badly to this music was exhausting! And then she saw Golden Arms approaching. He held his arms open to her.

Her clumsiness as a zydeco dancer didn't seem to bother him at all. He merely pressed her to him, so that her head was close to his smooth chest, exposed above his tank top. While the other dancers did a variety of complex movements and shimmies, Audrey and her partner just shuffled in place. She could see tufts of his strawberry-blond underarm hair. She sniffed him ecstatically. It had been months since she had been this close to a man.

When the dance was over, he stayed by her side, and when the band started a new song, he brought her to him again. And again. And again. They danced glued together. She was well acquainted with the texture and heft of his arms (satin over steel!) before she even found out his name. Audrey hoped that he was older than he looked. Maybe he was a young-looking thirty-five. That wouldn't be so bad. She inhaled him again and felt her legs grow limp. She would let him take her home and kiss her good night—but that was all. And if he asked her out, as of course he would (she had felt his erection for almost an hour), then she'd inquire about his age.

Having made these decisions, Audrey was very surprised when he squeezed her hand after the last dance and said, "It's been fun." Then he turned away and disappeared into the crowd.

Aroused and abandoned, Audrey sank into a chair. Well! What had that been about? Maybe she'd been away from the dating scene so long she had misread the signals. But how how many ways can you decode a hard-on? At the door she added her name to the mailing list and looked around for Golden Arms, but he was gone.

Still, she walked home elated. The night was clear and cold and she kept her coat open to cool off. If Richard didn't want her, someday others would. When her daughter Kimmy greeted her at the door and asked how the dance was, Audrey told her she'd had a good time. "I really like zydeco music," she said.

"What's that?"

"It's what they play in Louisiana—on accordion, fiddle, and washboard. Kind of folky, kind of funky, lots of fun.

The band sings in French and plays waltzes and two-steps and jitterbugs. It's all partner dancing."

"Did anyone ask you to dance, Mom?"

"Yes, sweetie. Is Jimbo asleep?" Jimbo was ten and Kimmy was fifteen. And Audrey, thinking of Golden Arms, felt about fifteen herself.

It was better to think about Golden Arms than to think about Richard and Irene all cozy in their Greenwich Village apartment. When he came by to visit the children, he looked pained and uncomfortable. Audrey observed this with some satisfaction: it was only right that he should feel guilty!

When she got a notice about the next zydeco dance, Audrey put it in the middle of her bulletin board. But the week before the dance, Audrey slipped on some ice and twisted her knee, damaging her anterior cruciate ligament. Her doctor put her in a leg immobilizer, a flexible removable cast that extended from ankle to mid-thigh. Wearing this white encasement on her left leg—over black pants for maximum contrast—she hobbled into the church basement. She had come by taxi because her leg made it difficult for her to drive.

The ticket taker said, "You must really like this music."

Audrey nodded vigorously, hypocritically. She cased the crowd. There he was! This time his tank top was blue and he was spinning a redhead around elaborately, now to one side, now to the other. But at the end of the dance he came to Audrey.

"Hi." He looked down at her and smiled, and the dimples came into his cheeks. He said with wonder, "You came."

Shy, Audrey only nodded.

"Can you dance?" he said, looking at her cast.

"The slow ones," said Audrey. A waltz was beginning.

"Well, save all the waltzes for me." He held out his hands.

And then it was like before, all ecstasy in his arms. Not fifteen, but *thirteen*, Audrey thought. Like the summer before eighth grade, when dances at the community center were her only sexual outlet. The more daring girls would let the boys "grind," and Audrey had acquired a reputation before she'd even been kissed.

When the dance was over, Golden Arms took Audrey home. Then he walked her to her door and kissed her on the front porch. It was a curiously immature kiss, like he was wiping jam from his mouth onto a napkin. But Audrey was so excited she could scarcely caw "good night," and she fumbled so badly with her house keys that she dropped them on the porch. He turned from the sidewalk to wave.

Kimmy opened the door and demanded, "Who was that?"

"His name is Tom."

"Isn't he a little young for you?"

"I don't know his age," said Audrey demurely.

She thought: now I have to explain myself to my daughter. She thought: now I have to explain myself to myself.

For she had never been drawn to younger men. She had always gone for men like Richard: dark-haired, older, remote, and successful. She was an English professor; Richard was a lawyer. Tom clerked in a music store and played in a zydeco band. She wondered how to explain a Tom in her life.

Looks, that was how.

But looks—surely *looks* weren't important to her! Perhaps, however, Tom's appeal went beyond appearance. Perhaps she was attracted to an essential sweetness that he seemed to radiate, a rough simplicity and decency, like a cowboy's.

My zydeco cowboy, she thought.

She wouldn't let him pick her up at home for fear of Kimmy's comments, so they met at a restaurant the next week. He was standing outside by the door in a beat-up brown leather jacket, his beautiful blond hair gleaming under a streetlight. He hugged her to him.

"Gosh, you're tall," she said.

"Six three."

"A foot taller than I am! We'll look ridiculous together."

"We will if we never stop smiling."

"You stop," she said.

"You."

Inside, she couldn't concentrate on the menu. She ordered what he did. Her cheeks ached from smiling and she felt stuck to the banquette.

"Perhaps we should learn a little about each other," began Audrey after the waiter left.

"Okay."

"I'm separated," she said. "My husband left in December."

"Was it a long marriage?"

Audrey nodded. No need to tell him how long.

"Do you think you'll get back together?"

Audrey shook her head. "Impossible. He's in love with somebody else. And he said our marriage was awful. The funny thing is, I thought it was pretty good." If this was so funny, why were there tears in her eyes?

Tom touched a tear as it eased down her cheek. He said, "Hey. Your marriage was probably fine. I bet he's just looking for a way to justify himself."

"You think?"

Tom nodded. "My girlfriend and I broke up three weeks ago. She lives in D.C., and I told her I didn't want a long-distance relationship. But that was just an excuse. And by then I'd met you."

"But you didn't even get my number!"

"It wouldn't have been right. Not when I was seeing her. Then I got so scared I wouldn't see you again." He looked down and turned pink.

A man who blushed! Audrey said, "Tom, I have to ask. How old are you?"

"Does it matter?" He put his hand over hers and she almost stopped breathing.

". . . just curious . . ." she croaked.

"I'm twenty-six."

"Oh my God!" Involuntarily, she pulled her hand back.

"What? How old are you?"

"Older" was all she could say.

"I thought you might be. So what?"

"Well, I have kids!"

"That's okay. How old are they?"

She mumbled, "Jimbo's ten. Kimmy's fifteen."

Tom nodded solemnly, taking it in. He said nothing at all.

Audrey swallowed. She might as well tell him the whole awful truth. "And there's Steve," she said miserably. "He's at college. He's eighteen."

He stared at her. *"You have an eighteen-year-old son?"*

"I started having kids very early," said Audrey—although twenty-four wasn't all *that* young. Tom looked shattered. She said, "Hey, it's okay. We can be friends."

"I don't want you for a friend."

Then they went back to smiling. Neither of them ate very much. After dinner they went to an action movie that didn't make much sense to her. Her concentration was on Tom's arm against hers, Tom's thumb against her palm.

After the movie, they parked—a block away from her house. When she put her hand under his jacket to touch his back, he actually trembled. Richard had been stolid, impassive, in bed and out. But with the smallest pressure of her hand upon his silken back, Tom moaned and gasped. What would he do if they actually went to bed?

This question gained urgency throughout the month of February. Her house was out of the question, inhabited as it was by her children, observed as it was by her neighbors. As for his house, which was in a town an hour north of hers, on their third date, when they were in the local diner, she discovered that he lived with his mother.

"But, Tom! You're a big boy now!" She smiled to make this a joke,

"I know. I really plan to move out. I moved back in after college, before I got a job. Then my dad got sick, and it was convenient to be home so I could help take care of him. When he died, Mom needed me. It works out. I do her chores, she does my meals and my laundry. I keep her company."

"You're a good son."

"I try."

Audrey returned to more pressing concerns. "Does your mom let you bring your friends home?"

"Sure. But I wouldn't feel right about women friends, about someone like you. . . ." He took a sip of his coffee. "She's Catholic. No sex without marriage. . . ."

"I don't want to have *sex* with you," Audrey said, sliding her leg against his under the table. "I just want to see what your room is like."

"My mom was really angry about my last girlfriend," said Tom. "The doctor in D.C."

"Angry?"

"Because she was thirty-six and divorced, with a kid. She thinks I should be with someone . . . less entangled. Not someone like you!"

Audrey listed her handicaps: "Three kids, no divorce papers yet—to say nothing about the age!"

"How old *are* you anyway?"

"To say nothing of the age," Audrey repeated. "Your poor mother. Her golden boy and all these older women!"

Audrey thought about Steve at college. What if he were

going out with a woman of thirty-four who had kids? Audrey would certainly be upset about that!

"What about your car?" asked Tom. He had a little economy model, but she had a station wagon. "Could you put down the backseat?"

"Are you crazy? Do you think I'd actually . . ."

"I guess that depends on how much you want me. . . ." He gave a lazy cowboy smile and Audrey felt her insides lurch.

"Not that much," she said. "I may have normal needs and urges, but I'm not a total slut!"

But before their next date, while the kids were in school, she put two quilts and two pillows in her car. When it was time to get dressed, she chose her clothes carefully: a soft sweater which buttoned up the front and a long, full skirt. She didn't wear a bra or tights, but she had to wear a slip so her skirt wouldn't stick to her legs. Under the slip, which was long and black, she wore a new pair of panties— emerald-green silk with two lace panels.

She met Tom at the movies, and afterward they parked by the tennis courts. They turned the radio to the country station, and to Patti Loveless they put down the backseat and spread the quilts on the flat area they'd created. She threw down the pillows. He went in through the back, and she closed the hatch. Then she got in through the front door and wriggled over the seat, muttering in mock exasperation, "The things I do for you!"

To her surprise, he was taking off his clothes: methodically removing his socks! He wriggled out of his pants. Then he pulled off his T-shirt. She unbuttoned her sweater, but she didn't actually remove any of her clothes. He took off all of his.

He didn't touch her until he was entirely naked between the two quilts. Then he hugged her and sighed. He held her breasts, one in each hand, and vibrated them. He buried his face in her neck.

Audrey kept thinking: I'm in the back of my car. In my own hometown! What if Richard saw me now? With each of Tom's wipe-the-jam kisses, Audrey let out a little moan. His hands were under her skirt now, touching her slip. He said, "Your skirt is so smooth."

She said, "It's not my skirt, it's my slip."

"Your legs are smooth, too," he said, stroking her thighs.

In response, she dug her nails into his back.

Her sense of hearing was shutting down, as it always did when she was excited. She could scarcely hear the radio: the song sounded faint and distorted, as if heard from underwater. Yes! It seemed like she was under warm water as Tom brought her hand down under the quilt to his very smooth, very hard—

A light was shining into the car.

"Tom, there's someone—

A policeman rapped against the window. Because the windows were electric and the engine was turned off, Audrey couldn't roll the window down and talk to him, so she had to button her sweater and slide ignominiously over the front seat. Then she opened the door and said, heart pounding, "Yes, Officer?"

By the streetlight, she could see his face—and wouldn't you know it, she recognized him! It was Bill Cavelli, the father of Jimbo's friend, Paul.

Officer Cavelli said, "I'm sorry, you'll have to move on. You can't do that here." He shone the light directly at her, then put it to one side. He asked incredulously, "Is that you, Audrey?"

"No," she said firmly. "I'm her sister, Patti, just visiting from out of town."

"Wow. You sure look alike."

"We're twins," Audrey said miserably.

He shone his light into the backseat. With the quilt up under his chin, Tom was pretending to sleep. He even let out a light snore.

Audrey said, "My friend is taking a nap."

"Uh-huh. Well, you'd better drive him somewhere else for his siesta."

"Yes, Officer. I will. Right away."

Officer Cavelli grinned. "And be sure to say hello to Audrey!"

"Don't tell her about this," said Audrey absurdly.

"It will be our secret."

She somehow doubted that. Cavelli went back to his car, and Audrey started her engine and drove away, muttering to Tom, "I can't believe this."

"God, you were cool," he said from the back as he pulled on his T-shirt. "Audrey's twin!"

"I don't think he bought it," said Audrey, adding crossly, "A lot of help you were, pretending to sleep!"

"What else could I do? Just be happy he didn't arrive five minutes later. We would have been doing it!"

Making love. Having sex. Getting it on. Fucking. So many ways to refer to intercourse, coitus, sexual relations! And she was dating a man who said "doing it."

"Tom, were you a fraternity boy?"

"You bet I was."

"A fraternity jock?"

He nodded enthusiastically; he had told her about his exploits in rugby and track.

"I would never have looked twice at you in college. I dated only intellectuals."

"You would never have looked twice at me in college," he said happily, "because I was still in elementary school!" He put his hand on the back of her neck.

Actually, by her calculations, when she started college,

Tom was still in diapers. What was she doing with this affectionate baby? Only having the time of her life!

She drove back to his car, by the movie theater, and she got out and freed him from the backseat.

"We can't go on like this," he said, stretching his tall body. "I'm dying for you, Audrey."

"Well, cars are out of the question!"

"What about my house? Next Saturday night?"

"What about your mother?"

"She's going away for the weekend. You could look at my athletic trophies!"

"Now, that's an idea. And since Richard's coming up to be with the kids, I could spend the whole night with you."

"Wow," said Tom. "That would be so cool." Sometimes he sounded younger than her son Steve.

Then he said, "Good night, my sweet beauty," and she fell to kissing him passionately.

Richard had never called her either beautiful or sweet. But maybe she hadn't been very sweet to him. In many ways, Richard had been tight and withholding, and she had, perhaps, responded in kind. With Tom, she felt another softer (wetter!) self emerge. Richard and Tom were such polar opposites, she sometimes imagined putting all of Richard's qualities into a computer and pressing an "opposite" button. Out would come Tom: friendly, musical, straightforward, young, tender, and financially impoverished.

The following Saturday it snowed, and Audrey watched the weather channel nervously. If it continued snowing, she wouldn't be able to drive up to Tom's, and God knew when they'd ever have the chance to go to bed again! At four, Richard came up from the city, by train and taxi. He and the children shoveled the paths even as it snowed. At five, the snow stopped, and at six she set out with her overnight bag. Five inches of snow had fallen.

"Where are you going anyway?" Richard asked.

"I'm visiting friends in Connecticut."

"Who?" he demanded.

"You don't know them." He glowered; she grinned.

She met Tom in a restaurant, because he said his house was hard to find. "Tom," she said over dessert. "Did you tell your mom you were having a guest?"

He drew his lower lip over his upper lip and shook his head, like a six-year-old who'd been caught stealing cookies.

"You should have told her, Tom. It's her house, after all."

"I know. But . . . I just couldn't. She'd want to know all about you."

"Well, we'll have to be *incredibly* careful. So she doesn't find out. Women notice the least little thing out of place in their homes. Like how the dish towel hangs or where the milk is replaced."

"We'll be very careful," said Tom. "And it will be worth it."

"How do you know?" she teased.

"Oh, Audrey!"

They left her car in town, so Tom's mother wouldn't see its tracks in the driveway. When they reached the house, he left the car first, and she followed carefully, stepping in his footprints. Thick snow lay everywhere; one of her high-heeled-boot prints could give them away.

They went into his room at once. The wallpaper had a railroad motif, and there was, indeed, a shelf full of athletic trophies. A well-used weight-lifting bench stood in one corner of the room, and a rack full of Cajun and zydeco CDs sat on his desk. Tom's high school graduation photo looked down from the wall. Audrey thought he'd barely changed since then.

Tom took off his clothes with incredible speed. Then he stood there, in the light, fully naked, exquisitely proportioned. His pubic hair was two shades deeper and redder than the hair on his head.

"Take off some clothes," he said to her.

She clicked on a desk lamp, turned off the overhead light, and walked toward him. "I'm shy," she said, craving his fumbling hands. "You do it."

It took him a while to take off her bra, but she didn't help him out because she was enjoying the process. He flung her bra onto his weight-lifting bench. Then he gazed awestruck at her breasts. He held them high in his hands, creating deep cleavage. "My God," he said. "You're so gorgeous."

Didn't he notice the cellulite on her thighs and the vertical lines on her forehead? Apparently not: he just kept looking and stroking and sighing. As for her, she couldn't stop touching Tom's astonishing skin, which covered astonishing muscles. It was as if he had just emerged from a lanolin bath, or as if he were a newborn, all soft from the womb.

Very soon he pushed her down on the bed and crawled on top of her. There hadn't been much foreplay—unless you counted the previous weeks—but Audrey was ready for him, and he slid right in. Ah, and it was not refined and not nuanced and not psychological at all! It was slam and slam and slam again: all-American fucking in position number one, which was, after all, what she loved most. She raised her legs a little and he just kept at it and at it, and now it was so sweet, so very wonderful that she heard herself sighing politely, "Oh, please."

He shoved deeper and harder and muttered, "You will!"

And then she did, murmuring, "Thank you, oh, thank you!" Wave after wave, and all over him.

Only after the last little wavelet had receded did he change his rhythm, shifting into the higher gear he apparently needed. At first, Audrey was so lost in her own after-pleasure that she scarcely noticed Tom, but after a while she opened her eyes to see him over her, eyes closed in seemingly agonized concentration. A drop of sweat fell from his face onto hers, and strange loud sounds emerged from his throat. She reached down to where their bodies met, and kept her hand there while he opened his eyes and actually, wordlessly, screamed—so that she feared for her eardrums. He yelled additionally, "I'm coming. I'M COMING!" He thrashed for many seconds, then put his head in her neck and was still.

Wow! She'd had no idea this ebullient intensity was in the male repertoire! It was lucky he lived in a single-family house: if this had been an apartment, someone next door, hearing Tom's scream, might have thought he was being murdered. Perhaps he yelled "I'm coming" so that no one would think he was dying.

Soon he was utterly relaxed. With his blond hair, smooth skin, and Norse features, he looked like an angel asleep in her arms. She reached one arm over the side of the bed to find her panties. For this occasion, she had chosen the green silk panties again, but she didn't think he'd even seen them—he'd just pulled them off impatiently. Now, with minimum movement so that he would stay sleeping, she slipped them back on, to catch any seepage.

For all she knew, Tom's mother made his bed!

The desk light was still on, for which she was grateful. With any luck, she wouldn't sleep at all! He looked so lovely there beside her, and it had been so long since she'd been in bed with a man, she didn't want to lose a single minute to Morpheus! She wanted to stay in a fugue state all night, in joyous and conscious oblivion with Tom.

Soon, however, Audrey felt herself drifting into a doze. She forced her eyes open to look at her lover. She saw only his peaceful profile. Then she raised herself onto one elbow to look at him full-face. His reddish-blond eyelashes curled on his cheeks, his muscled arm was raised, revealing his thrilling armpit. Men's looks had never much mattered to her before: indeed, this had been a point of pride. But Tom's face was beautiful, especially in repose, and she was ashamed to realize that now it did matter after all.

But why should she be ashamed? If you love a man for his wit, your love is renewed every time he says something amusing. But if you love a man for his beauty, merely setting eyes on him makes you love him anew. And what's wrong with that?

Love! she mocked herself. One good fuck and you're thinking it's love! She gave a tiny, self-deprecating "hunf."

He opened his baby-blue eyes and said, "Hi."

"Hi."

"What are you doing?"

"I'm watching you sleep."

"You are?"

She nodded.

"Oh, Audrey." And then he was touching her again. His hands soon discovered her panties upon her. He murmured, "Why did you put on your panties?"

He slurred the "t" so it sounded like "pannies," a mispronunciation she had always found inexplicably exciting. She didn't want to go into the issue of bedsheets and laundry, so she merely said, "I thought we were through for the night."

"Hell, no," said her cowboy, tugging them off and climbing aboard.

This time she was the noisy one, as if she'd finally been given permission to let go. And—like Monica Seles's grunts during tennis—making noise during sex did seem to heighten the action! After orgasm she chided herself: what a thing to be thinking of, Monica Seles! Then she fell asleep, almost instantly.

The next time she woke up, the room was black: Tom

must have turned off the desk lamp. She was glad it was still dark outside: perhaps she hadn't been asleep for more than a few minutes and she had hours left to enjoy sharing the bed. She reached her arm over his back, and, seemingly from sleep, he said, "Audrey" and flung an arm over her. How warm and friendly he was, this Tom! How appreciative! In appreciation herself, she began to stroke his back, and she told herself it was lucky she was so well sated, because otherwise, merely touching this man would probably arouse her. Indeed, to her astonishment, she was actually getting excited again, but she knew it was insane, and she hoped he wouldn't misinterpret (i.e., interpret correctly) her increasingly ardent caresses. He would think she was insatiable.

Insatiable! Now even her thoughts were getting her hot: he had turned her into a sex machine!

Needless to say, this notion turned her on too.

Because he was sighing in his sleep, she sent one assessing, caressing hand down. He was rigid and ready. It was only charitable to help him relax into sleep again.

Sweet charity. This time she was on top, but he insisted on his rhythm. After a while she called out his name, a cry torn from her body, and he groaned out hers.

Then it was dawn: gray streaked with salmon. Audrey tiptoed to the bathroom, which he shared with his mother, and peed quietly. She wanted a fresher mouth, in case he wanted to kiss her, but she didn't want to go back into his room and risk waking him up while she fumbled for her toiletries kit in her overnight bag, so she squeezed some toothpaste onto her finger, being careful to press the tube where a dent already was. You couldn't be careful enough in another woman's house!

She crept back to Tom's room and slid under the covers again. Audrey calculated that by now Richard had been seeing his girlfriend for eight months. Audrey very much doubted that *they* made love more than once a night! He hadn't done so with Audrey past their first month together, and he'd been in his twenties then. Now he was almost fifty: twenty-three years older than Tom! Would she ever stop comparing the two—or measuring her life against Richard's? Perhaps not, and this briefly depressed her, although the whole sky was rosy.

Tom said, "You're awake."

She nodded.

"What are you thinking of?"

She didn't want to say "Richard," so she said, "The dawn."

He seemed disappointed, so she added, "Beginnings."

"You sweet thing," he said. "I was wondering . . ." He brought her hand down.

"Tom! I don't believe this! You're faking it!" she said absurdly.

"That would be quite a trick. Do you think we could . . ."

She wanted to tell him she was all worn out, but she didn't want to remind him, even indirectly, of how much older she was than he. Instead, she scolded him gently: "Haven't you had enough?"

"Apparently not. You just excite me so much."

"I don't know why."

"I don't know why either. What am I going to do?"

"I'll push it down," she said, attempting to so, but of course this didn't work. "And now you'll forget all about it."

She removed her hand, and he replaced it with his. Then he was moving his fingers up and down. Right in front of her! She was dually amazed: at his need and at his boldness. She didn't think she could touch herself in front of anybody else, but her presence didn't deter him at all. Thinking she could learn what would please him best from watching him at work, she flung down the sheet to check out his technique. He used his thumb and third and fourth fingers, fluttering his index irregularly here and there.

"Oh, let me," Audrey heard herself saying, and she pushed his hand away and did the same moves on him while his breath grew hoarse.

With her other hand she caressed his testicles.

"Oh my God!" he hollered, shooting upward, upon her.

They lay grinning side by side, equally proud.

Later, she shared his shower and his towel, so there wouldn't be one extra used one. She cleaned the hairs from the drain so Tom's mother wouldn't find her long, dark ones and know Tom had had company. Audrey worried that the very cleanliness of the drain might be a giveaway, but perhaps before Tom's mother looked, Tom would take a shower and there would be some short blond hairs, as usual, for her to find.

She got dressed in fresh clothes, then she asked, "Most days, do you make your bed?"

"Nah, I just kind of pull up the bedclothes."

"Then do it," she said, and he did.

Downstairs, although they were both very hungry, she cooked only two eggs for them both, in case Tom's mother was counting. Audrey didn't think slices of bread would be counted. Still, four was a large part of a loaf, so they had two slices from one open, frozen loaf of sliced wheat and two from some fresh pumpernickel. She had only a sip of his orange juice. She loaded Tom's plates and utensils into the dishwasher and washed her own by hand, giving them to Tom to dry and put away.

Throughout breakfast and cleanup, Tom gazed at her as if she were a goddess.

"You look so dazzled," she said.

"I am. I can't believe I'm dating a beautiful, sexy professor—who's doing my dishes!"

"And I can't believe I'm dating at all—yet alone a young zydeco cowboy!"

"What a torrid night that was," said Tom.

Torrid! That was not a word she expected from him. Perhaps he had depths she hadn't realized. Audrey looked at him fondly. She said, "And we've been so incredibly careful, your mom will never find out!"

Just before leaving, she ran upstairs to check the bedroom and bathroom one last time. She checked the kitchen again too. As they walked down the snow-covered path, she stepped in his footprints as before.

Driving home down the parkway, she sang all the way to her exit. Some of the songs she sang had been popular before Tom was born.

When they met at the diner the following week, Audrey could tell something was wrong before she even got out of the car. Tom looked very young, very nervous, hunched into himself. She said "Tom?" and walked toward him.

"Oh, Audrey." He held her against him very hard. He put his nose in her hair and sighed. A sharp wind was blowing; he gave her a little push toward the diner, and they went inside and sat at a booth.

"What is it?" asked Audrey, taking off her coat. He left his leather jacket on.

"I had this big fight with my mom."

"Really? About what?"

"About last weekend. Like, are these yours?" He reached into his jacket pocket and brought out her green silk panties.

Audrey stared at them in astonishment. Then she took them from him and pushed them into her handbag. "I don't understand," she said slowly. "Where did you *get* these?"

Tom said, "Mom found them in the bed when she was changing the sheets. Audrey, it isn't funny!"

For Audrey had burst into gales of laughter. "I'm sorry,

I'm sorry," she spluttered. "But when you think of how careful we were about every last thing—how scrupulous—" For a minute she couldn't continue. Then she burst out, "And then we left this, the most obvious, incontrovertible sign that you'd brought home a woman to bed!" Audrey was off again.

Tom grumbled, "I'm glad you think it's so funny. I told Mom I was going to move out."

"All because of my panties?"

"One thing led to another."

"Well, Tom. It's not so terrible. You're twenty-six. It's time you were out on your own."

"I guess." For a while he was silent. Then he took off his jacket and said, "You know, maybe I'll look for a place in your town. It's closer to work than my mom's. I could see you more often. And we'd have a place to be alone."

"That sounds good," said Audrey. She thought of Richard: of his general gloom, of his middle-aged angst, of his ultimate betrayal. Tom watched her attentively, his golden hair curling on his forehead. Audrey said, "Maybe it's all for the best."

Tom frowned. "Audrey, did you leave them there on purpose?"

"My panties? Of course not! God, how can you say that? After I was so careful about everything else!"

"Yeah, but . . . like, you really wanted me to move out, didn't you? So maybe unconsciously . . ."

Audrey considered the idea. It was just within the realm of possibility . . .

Tom reached for her hand across the Formica table, "It's okay," he said. He pressed his thumb against her palm.

Audrey said slowly, "You mean, like a Freudian slip . . . ?"

"Not a Freudian *slip*," Tom said, grinning. "Freudian *pannies*."

The Pleasures of the Text

MY MOTHER AND MY STEPFATHER were kissing on the couch. This wasn't unusual: Nina and Marius had a passionate marriage. But Bethany, my new friend, was shocked.

"Do they do that a lot?" she asked when we were in my room.

"Sure. Don't *your* parents ever kiss?"

"Not like that," said Bethany.

She told everyone in the eighth grade about my sexy mother and her handsome Belgian husband—and how cavalier I was about their lust. Rumor had it that Marius was not my mother's second husband, but her fourth or fifth. Rumor had it that he wasn't her husband at all—but her lover! Rumor had it that they did it right in front of me that I didn't mind. Of course they didn't, and of course I did.

Because although I never saw them making love, I often

heard them at it, and that was bad enough. Sometimes from their room at night, a rhythmic, slapping noise reached mine. No cries of pain: just slapping. I knew that they were having sex, yet I had never read that sex and slapping went together. If I heard the sound of hand on flesh—his hand, her flesh, I never doubted—I would reach under my bed for my transistor radio and put it near my ear, so that the music of love's frustration ("You Really Got a Hold on Me," "Half-way to Paradise") replaced the sounds of its satisfaction. But why were they getting satisfied like that? Was punishment part of the pleasure? It was all known and unknown to me, obvious and baffling, appalling and inflaming.

I knew that no one would tell me about all of this, and if there were books on the subject, how was I ever to find them? Surely, no librarian would help me here. Indeed, I feared that any decent librarian, knowing of my researches, would call up the vice squad at once. (The vice squad was another dangerous and exciting notion: jeering men who chased you down and locked you up when you were *bad*.)

Deprived of my usual resources, people or books, I could find no answers to my questions about pleasure and humil-iation, so I began telling myself tales that combined the two to best effect. At night I would lie in bed, open-eyed, vaguely watching how the passing cars outside changed the pattern of light and shadow on my ceiling as I carefully com-posed my vignettes. The theme was always the same; the plot varied but slightly; but the telling could always be dif-ferent—and better.

It didn't take me long to discover certain rules. The story worked best when you saved all the good parts for later: you couldn't have him slapping and stroking her buttocks right away. First you had to have the stuff about him chasing her though the apartment—no, you had to have the reason they were there in the first place, why she was running from him, you had to establish their connection. Some nights I fell asleep before anything interesting happened because it took so long to get the background information right. Once that was achieved, then I had to describe things: the clothing she started out by wearing, the furniture she desperately placed between them in her pathetic attempts to avoid her fate, the geography of the apartment.

If I needed specificity of motive, wardrobe, and locale, I needed anonymity of character. My men and women were always a blur. Perhaps delicacy and horror forbade me to people my fantasies with anyone I knew—even while (I now see) I needed the possibility that the man might be Marius and the woman my mother or myself. So the characters in my reveries were faceless and nameless.

Even though I never wrote down these stories, I chose my words with care. Euphemisms pleased me more than dirty words: he never asked her to "suck his cock"; he requested her to "worship his manhood." He never said, "I'm going to fuck you"; he whispered, smiling, "Now I'll explore your adorable body." The word "adorable" thrilled me. The man called her his adorable pet or his adorable plaything or his adorable little girl.

One of the subtler pleasures of this nighttime activity was the mental exercise involved. I had to remember where I was going; I had to make constant choices about how to get there; I had to compose and criticize at the same time; I was author and audience throughout. Furthermore, once I had gotten each sentence right, I had to memorize it exactly so that I could "read" the final version, slowly, for my delectation.

Night after night I indulged myself thus in narration, my hands chastely folded behind my neck, my eyes searching the shadows for the perfect words. These were my first short stories, and I had high standards, considering my subject matter. My aesthetics were lofty; my mind, in the gutter.

One day, at a sex education film in school, I learned that

when women got sexually excited, their "genitals"—awful word!—swelled and got wet. That night, purely in the spirit of scientific inquiry, I tested myself before and after my narrative effort. No doubt about it! All these months, I'd been arousing myself—mentally!

It never occurred to me that there was any other way to do it.

One night when my parents were out, I climbed upon a kitchen stool to investigate some old books on a high shelf in the living room. My mother had minored in psychology at college, and I saw many dusty books with crumbling covers. One title engaged my interest: *Frigidity in Women* by Friedrich Stekel. I pulled the fat book down. It was old and dry with yellowing pages: boring, with diagrams. I turned to the chapter on techniques to overcome frigidity, and as I was leafing through, I came across an interesting idea. The man could make the woman have an orgasm just by rhythmically rubbing his penis against her clitoris (which seemed to be on the outside "down there"). If a penis would do, why not a hand, and, if a hand, why not mine?

I went to bed early that night, eager for experiment. I put my hand between my legs—but soon withdrew it. The sticky feeling on my fingers was unpleasant and distracting; my hand wasn't "other" enough. I tried again, on top of my pajamas. This way, my hand was happier, and I worked on finding a rhythm. Soon I found one that was very nice, it just got better and better, I couldn't believe how good it was, my whole body seemed brimming and breathless, ecstatic, when—oh! how sad! One sharp convulsion, and another, and another. It was over. Exhausted and astounded, I fell asleep at once.

The entire next day, I looked forward to bedtime with all the eagerness of a voluptuary with a new concubine. At night I said I was too tired to play Scrabble with my mother and certainly too tired to play chess with Marius. Playing chess with Marius meant seeing how long I could stave off the inevitable loss. I always felt plucky to be playing him at all, and I considered I'd done well if it took more than twenty minutes before he said "checkmate," or "checka-matta." Whether "checka-matta" was the proper term in one of the seven languages he spoke or an invention of his own, I never knew, but that was what he said when he'd devised an especially tricky mate, a comically quirky resolution to the game. The looks we exchanged after he said "checka-matta"—my blushing recognition of his superior wits, his pride of victory mingled with commiseration for my defeat—were as intimate as any we shared.

I said, "I'm really too tired for chess."

"Well, at least listen to this lovely Bach concerto with us," said Marius.

I shook my head and yawned. Good night, then! Kiss for Marius, kiss for my mother. Into my room. Into my pajamas. Out with the light. Under the covers. Ah, like that, like that. Slow down, now. Climax ends it all, *slow down*. It's the moments just before you want, yes those, like that, oh, no! Shudder after empty shudder.

By the third night, I was already getting bored with the proceedings. I stopped and started, to prolong things, but my mind was restless, there was nothing to fix it on, and while I was wondering where to focus—*boing*, like a stretched rubber band rudely plucked, I thrummed once unpleasantly, and it was all over—without that splendid soaring feeling just before.

This was terrible. Had I already exhausted the intense and easy pleasure my chance discovery had promised? Was it going to be three times and out? Were my greatest physical experiences behind me—at the age of thirteen? Was this why no one had ever told me you could bring youself bliss—because they knew it soon wore out and left you ever after disappointed?

The next night, I went to bed at my usual time and re-solved to go to sleep at once. Maybe if I gave myself a rest, I could someday give myself that great feeling once more. But "someday" was remote, and just remembering that great feeling made me sort of feel it again, and want more of it right away. And my hand was so close, it was such a temp-tation. And I was so wide awake. How else was I ever to sleep?

So I began building up pleasure again. And it was okay, but soon I was facing what now seemed to be "that old problem" of what to do with my mind. Suddenly I had a startling idea. I was so surprised and intrigued that my hand stopped moving entirely. What if I told myself one of my bedtime stories *while I touched myself*? That would surely occupy my mind!

In the interest of science, I decided that I had to get calm again before trying out my idea, so I turned on my lamp and rearranged my bookshelf. When everything was tidy and in order, I went back to bed and turned off the light. I opened my legs, ready to learn what mental and physical pleasure, combined, might yield. He began chasing her through the apartment, saying, "You can't escape, my ador-able girl . . ."

Oh, *God*. It was right away apparent, and became ever more so, that I had stumbled onto a brilliant solution to my problem.

The next morning, before brushing my teeth, I stared at my reflection with fascination and awe, as if facing genius.

By the time I found out about the slapping, learned after his death that—at his insistence—it was *her* hand and *his* flesh, I was in my twenties, and it was too late.